"Put me down, Sean!" Taylor demanded, as he lifted her high in the air.

"Kiss me first," he growled, in his Frankenstein voice.

"No way, Buster Brown," Taylor said, twisting from side to side in his arms. "No kisses here!"

"Then no lunch," he threatened.

"Lemme down, you big Irish bully!" They were beginning to attract a crowd. Taylor shrieked as Sean started tickling her knees.

"Okay, okay," she surrendered, "but keep it clean or the deal's off."

His eyes were much too triumphant. They locked with hers as he began to lower her down along his body. Holding her at face level, he smiled.

"Well, see if you like this!" He kissed her, her legs still dangling. Then she could feel nothing but the hot rush of feeling and desire. . . .

WHAT ARE *LOVESWEPT* ROMANCES?

They are stories of true romance and touching emotion. We believe those two very important ingredients are constants in our highly sensual and very believable stories in the *LOVESWEPT* line. Our goal is to give you, the reader, stories of consistently high quality that may sometimes make you laugh, sometimes make you cry, but are always fresh and creative and contain many delightful surprises within their pages.

Most romance fans read an enormous number of books. Those they truly love, they keep. Others may be traded with friends and soon forgotten. We hope that each *LOVESWEPT* romance will be a treasure—a "keeper." We will always try to publish

LOVE STORIES YOU'LL NEVER FORGET
BY AUTHORS YOU'LL ALWAYS REMEMBER

The Editors

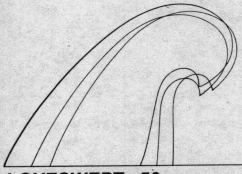

LOVESWEPT • 56

Kimberli Wagner
Encore

BANTAM BOOKS
TORONTO • NEW YORK • LONDON • SYDNEY • AUCKLAND

ENCORE

A Bantam Book / August 1984

Bantam Books are published by Bantam Books, Inc. Its trademark, consisting of the words "Bantam Books" and the portrayal of a rooster, is Registered in U.S. Patent and Trademark Office and in other countries. Marca Registrada. Bantam Books, Inc., 666 Fifth Avenue, New York, New York 10103.

PRINTED IN THE UNITED STATES OF AMERICA

O   0 9 8 7 6 5 4 3 2 1

One

"Johnny," Taylor said distractedly, "I don't have time for bad jokes. I'm stuck in the middle of these rewrites."

With the phone glued to one shoulder, Taylor searched through the wild topknot of her hair for one of the three pencils she *knew* were stuck there, dammit, while she shuffled notes with her other hand. Suddenly she saw the page she'd been looking for and dropped the phone as she went under the cluttered desk for it.

"Hold on!" she yelled in the general direction where she thought the phone had landed.

Johnny gave her thirty seconds after he heard a gleeful "Ah, *hah!*" then he started yelling into the receiver, his bushy white eyebrows dancing furiously.

When he heard laughter, he knew she had picked up the phone and was letting him yell himself out. It was a trick she had used successfully before. As soon as the volume level decreased, she stuck the phone back in the crook of her shoulder, just in time to hear him mutter something about ". . . and all for a lousy fifteen percent!"

Still laughing, she got out, "Well, Johnny, just what *did* you want?"

This, quite naturally, set off another volley of imprecations that had Taylor clutching the back of her chair for support.

Now, another, softer soul, might have been a bit nervous, if not frightened, listening to the fluency and imagination with which the man used words. Certainly the range of volume and pitch issuing from the receiver *could* be intimidating.

But Taylor Neal was a great lover of theatricality. And John Byner O'Malley was an Irish master of both it and the English language. He was also the best agent in New York; she was sure of it. He had been hers since her first Off-Off Broadway production, nearly eight years before.

Suddenly recalled to his original mission, O'Malley said with unusual severity, "Seriously, luv, no joke, we've a bit of a problem."

"So shoot, O'Malley," Taylor returned as she sat back down and pulled clean paper to make notes, pencil ready.

Clearing his throat, O'Malley started enumerating, very much in his usual style.

"One, when you were married to Sean O'Brien"—he took a breath—"you shared power of attorney, did you not?"

At the dagger sound of that name, Taylor had become quite still except for a sudden increase in pulse rate. She didn't like the sound of this, not a bit.

"What's this all about, Johnny?" Was that her voice?

"As I *tried* to tell you before," he went on with exaggerated patience—ever the martyr—"I'm holding the backers' contract for *The Run*. And I'll tell you plain, luv, it looks like we're stuck."

Yes, her stomach was definitely falling.

"Go on," she said steadily.

"This contract was signed over a year ago by Sean on behalf of the both of you. It states—wait till you hear *this*—that you're to star and O'Brien's to direct." He paused at her gasp. "I suppose it seemed a good idea at the time."

"I'm dying, O'Malley, I'm dying."

He went on resolutely. "Two, your backers want their five hundred thousand dollars back unless we comply. I don't know why they're suddenly sticking so hard, when they hadn't said a word. But they are, and they've a right."

"Oh, my God . . ."

"Aye, and there's more. These dear, darlin' boys—where did we get them from, anyhow?— well, they seem to have contacted O'Brien with the same ultimatum. They're holding him responsible for half the money."

"But it's already invested in the production!"

"Oh, don't think they don't know that. But they want what they want. And they want the both of you or the money."

At this her eyes closed in defeat.

"Now, hold tight, luv. I spoke to Sean this morning."

"Oh? And?" That just couldn't be her own voice.

"And he's on his way back from filming in England. There's an editing delay, and he's agreed to the terms, uhm, conditionally." The next part he tried to get out as quickly as possible.

"He . . . wants in on the rewrites, and he wants to stay at the brownstone for the duration." There was dead silence on the line. "Taylor, luv . . . uh, you all right, there?"

A moment passed. Then: "Later, O'Malley" was all he got for his pains before the phone was disconnected.

Taylor sat, her hand gripping the phone for moments out of time, feeling nothing. Then, still numb, she headed down the stairs to the living room, scattering papers like confetti in her wake.

At last, in front of the bar stand, she reached for what she assumed packed the strongest wallop, and splashed a killing dose of Jack Daniels into a glass. She didn't even notice how her hand was shaking.

"Ugh." She grimaced after the too-large gulp. "Poison! I guess this'll do it."

Then her feet took her to the couch, where she sank down and gave herself up to the images running through her mind.

O'Brien! He was a six-foot-four "Black Irish" man whose presence carried quite as much weight as his husky frame. He was square-jawed and always a bit tan, but it was those blue eyes that gave him unfair advantage. He was also a terrifically talented stage director. And he'd been the director of Taylor's first Broadway production, her first important lead. From the first day of rehearsal, she'd known he was trouble.

She had been an hour early for the initial reading of the play. For nearly half an hour she was alone in the dim netherworld of backstage. Then familiar and unfamiliar faces began to trickle in. Sammy, an old sailor of a stage manager, was one. He had stage-managed Taylor's first Off Broadway show and had stopped her backstage after opening night to say, "This show's gonna fold soon, girlie, but don't *you* give up."

His simple generosity and kindness made them fast friends—of the backstage sort—and they had worked together twice more since. They caught up on family news, her mother, his grand-children, and had begun discussing the promise of this new project and Taylor's good fortune in land-ing the lead when it happened.

She and Sammy stood between the curtain's ropes and sandbags, chattering away about every-thing and nothing as people settled themselves, when she felt a mild frisson running down her spine. Turning nervously to look behind her, she saw what had caused it.

There he stood, eyeing her speculatively, up, down, and around. An actor, she was sure, but a gorgeous giant of a man for all that. Tall, very tall, and football-athletic, he had a magnetic, dark sort of sexiness that Taylor couldn't help but feel. His strong, angular features could only work together with a man his size. Everything about him was big and dark, but for his blue, blue eyes. Eyes that were locked on her at this moment.

Now, Taylor knew that her five-foot six-inch frame looked pretty good in rehearsal clothes. Per-haps her lacy peasant blouse showed a bit too much white shoulder, and her old jeans *did* fit a mite snug. But this redhead could feel every inch of her own skin under those bright eyes—and it wasn't the most comfortable feeling in the world. In any case, this guy was overdoing the technique!

She had to laugh, forcing his eyes to hers. He looked like a boy with both hands caught in the cookie jar.

Watching the interchange, Sammy must have felt his responsibility, and dutifully introduced them.

Sean O'Brien, devil that he was, greatly enjoyed watching her face when Taylor learned just *who* he was. Watching her blush wildly, O'Brien gave a slow nod, nicknamed her "Red"—as if he had a right!—and turned away to business.

She *hated* being called Red, and she was sure he knew it! Oh, this was going to be just great, and why did she feel as though she'd just been set up?

She was already steaming when she sat down at the long table with her script. And after watching Sean O'Brien do a charming introduction of himself and his ideas about the play, Taylor stiffened her spine for trouble. She knew both the play and the playwright. She had read the script months before and had already formed some strong conclusions about her role in it. Their differences of opinion were obvious, even in a first reading.

When O'Brien asked her to stay after the reading, she was wary, but he neither made a pass nor laughed at her ideas. He simply listened with complete concentration, raised a few salient points of his own, and nodded. She didn't know whether that nod of his charmed or annoyed her, but the man did charge up the air.

"Tell you what," he said seriously, looking her straight in the eye. "You try it my way and I'll try it yours, and we'll see what kind of pie we decide on."

She echoed his nod with a slow one of her own. "Deal."

Then he held out his hand with a big, open smile. "Red"—he didn't seem to notice her wince—"this is going to be a pleasure." He turned to the darkness behind them to yell over one shoulder. "Sammy, lock up, will you? I'm an hour late!"

"Sure thing, Sean. See you tomorrow," came back from the shadows. Then he turned back to her, measuring something in her face.

"Eight o'clock tomorrow!" he reminded her sternly—as if she needed reminding—before he started for the backstage door. So much for charm. Without slowing his stride, he said casually, "I'm headed downtown. Need a lift?"

"No, thanks," she answered just as casually, wondering if that was the pass. The cocky grin that overcame him seemed to read her mind, but she didn't care. Let him take it as a warning. So she *was* attracted to him. So what?

Throughout four weeks of rehearsals, that attraction remained unspoken and under cover. She kept waiting for him to make fatal mistakes, like fondling an actress to get better work or attention, or insensitivity when someone was having a hard time. He wasn't above temperament if it helped him get what he wanted, but he always played fair. Carefully, brilliantly, with intelligence and humor, he constructed the workings of a good show by bullying and cajoling, somehow bringing out the best in nearly everyone. She didn't always agree with his interpretation of a scene, and there were some colorful arguments, but if she really wanted to take issue, he would always listen. And, quite often, change his mind.

Very dangerous.

After another week she wondered if the chemistry between them remained unacknowledged out

7

of some idea of professional ethics or if he was somehow attached, but by this time she was too embarrassed to ask Sammy or anyone else in the cast. And all her speculations disappeared the day he came into the backstage shower as she was hurrying out, both of them barely covered in the hotel-style theater towels.

His hands automatically grabbed her shoulders as she barreled right into him. *She* steadied herself with her hands against his chest. *Their* towels were a mutual loss. His grip tightened as she bent to retrieve hers, and her head snapped up reflexively.

That was the mistake.

She was caught by those deep blue eyes and never even knew what hit her until she was in the middle of the absolutely best and most magical kiss she'd ever, ever had.

Her arms went by themselves—she'd have sworn—up and around those great shoulders as if they'd done it a thousand times before. And his hands ran slowly down her sides, over her ribs, as if they, too, were completely familiar to him.

Finally he pulled his head back a fraction. Taylor could only look downward as she panicked. What was she *doing*! And, to make matters worse, her body was betraying her badly, and he *had* to feel the most obvious ways in which it was. But then, so was his, at *least* as obviously!

Then she had to laugh, except that it came out as a sort of strangled giggle, which, of course, infected O'Brien.

Fighting for control, they slowly came unglued, and both reached for the same towel. Harrumphing like two old college professors, they finally got their mantles sorted out and draped accordingly.

Her dimples delighted him so much that he suddenly made a decision, one that he had long debated.

"Now we've definitely crossed the line," he said as he wiped her tearing eyes gently with his thumbs, hands cradling her cheeks.

"What line?" She was still insensible.

"This line." And he replaced his thumbs with butterfly kisses from the softest mouth, finally leading down to her own, seeking deeply, with an unerringly spectacular entrance.

Her hands moved restlessly over the soft hair covering his warm chest. Her finger found his small, hard nipples, and he responded with a start of surprise and arousal.

She was fascinated by the flush that ran up his neck and over his face under his tan. That she could affect him so deeply, with a single touch, gave her a hard pain of her own in a region down below.

Wild, she felt like a wild thing, she realized as she let her hands become acquainted with the shape and form of his hips, then meet at his spine.

Every bit of her body seemed so full. And every place his hands touched seemed to take on a life of its own.

Then her hands were moving by instinct, nails running tantalizingly up his back; over hard muscles and tightened skin they ran down again.

Behind her, his fingers kneaded the soft flesh under her towel, measuring shape and contour. He pressed her to him, lifting her to her toes for a better fit, and buried his hot face in her neck with a low groan.

"Yes, Red, yes," he whispered huskily just over her ear. Such passion in a mere whisper! And, as Taylor felt him gently biting at her neck, she knew nothing was ever going to be as good as this. Heat surged through her.

Suddenly, knowing just what she wanted, Taylor pulled away and grabbed O'Brien's big hand, locking the bathroom door with one flick of the wrist.

Somehow unsure, now that she'd committed herself, she peeked through her lashes at the big man standing beside her. But the heat of his look urged her on. She tugged at the hand she held to pull him along with her, and didn't mind a bit that towels had begun to slide again.

In those few seconds Taylor could remember every accidental touch between them. She thought of the way O'Brien would toss his dark head back when he was describing a scene. And she could still feel that special frisson down her spine that said he was watching her when she wasn't looking.

He was thinking, similarly, of how long and how much he had wanted this green-eyed witch. And as he followed her lead, he remembered the first time he'd seen her. The way she had caught him staring and had laughed right in his face, her wild red hair startling in the backstage lighting. And he was glad, quite glad, she was here with him now. He wouldn't think of consequences; he could only think of now, this minute, this woman.

"You wanted a shower, sir?" she asked shakily in her sweetest Cockney. She looked quite like an underaged street waif, too, with her eyes wide and round, and her wet hair clinging.

Her head was lifted proudly, as if she were afraid of what she might hear in response. But

there was answer enough as he reached to sur-
round her in his arms, nearly squeezing the very
life from her. Still holding her tightly, he turned
the taps, then reached behind her for the bottle of
liquid soap, and quirked an unholy grin.

He mesmerized her as he upended the bottle in
his hand and trailed the creamy soap down from
her shoulders.

Moving oh, so slowly now, he replaced the bottle on the shelf behind them and, just as carefully,
began sculpting her body with only hands and
soap.

Taylor had never in her life made the sounds
she heard herself making then, as his hands ran
over her. Her head fell back slightly as her lips
parted, leaving O'Brien practicing new exercises in
control.

Pushing her gently back into the warm
streams of water, he leaned to kiss her. One hand
cradled the back of her head, the other curved over
a hip finally to find that place that ached most for
him.

Lord, but the man could kiss, and how she
wanted this, wanted him.

Moving closer to him, she was suddenly frantic
with the need to rush onward, to fill her mouth
with the taste of him. Reaching high around his
neck, she lifted herself, locking her elbows and
tasting, biting everywhere her mouth could find
him.

Holding her against him by the waist, her feet
brushing the tops of his, he continued to touch her
intimately, reveling in her response. As he felt her
come closer to the feelings he wanted for her, he
lowered her back to the ground, kissing her hungrily. And so soon, so soon it happened.

Time stopped when he did, his hands now covering both breasts. Blue eyes met green with a wordless message, and the only sound was that of ragged breathing.

"Yes," he said, in a low, gritty voice, compelling a response.

"Yes," she answered, with a smile that was beyond anything.

This was a man to care about; a man *she* could care about. Kissing her again with that warm, wonderful mouth, he backed her against one wall. He ran his hands slowly down her spine. Then, curving over, under, he lifted her with both hands and settled her beautifully.

"O'Brien . . . Ooooooh Brien," she cried as she wrapped her legs around his strong back.

"Dear God, what am I doing to myself?" Taylor said aloud, jolting herself from memories that were, after almost three years, still much too vivid.

She took another gulp of bourbon, detesting bourbon, and forced her thoughts to memories only a year old, and less than pleasant.

Married a year and a half, she and O'Brien had lived in the Greenwich Village brownstone her grandmother had left her. Another successful production, their second together, was finished, and Taylor had begun to work on an idea she had for a play. Sean, in the meantime, was supportive, but already at work rehearsing a new play of his own.

It was the first time they had really been separated, professionally or personally, and the first time they had to maintain conflicting schedules. There were growing pains.

Those schedules differed terribly, and weekends simply didn't exist when each was working on his own timetable or had problems in production.

Always before they had had work in common to discuss. Production disasters, cast or personality conflicts, or script problems were breakfast fare. Suddenly they were both deprived of confidante and best friend.

O'Brien rehearsed at all hours and had production and script-revision meetings and special rehearsals in his "free" time.

Taylor had her own production meetings, plus those with agents, casting agents, actors, backers. And she wasn't even in production yet! *Her* free time was spent glued to the typewriter, writing different versions of the play. It was her first, and she was determined that it should be noticed and that it should be good.

Their friends were understanding, but things were not so easy at home. Tempers were overtaxed, and breakfasts were often quiet.

Though she had hired a cleaning woman and retired from her social life, Taylor had really thought of it as simply a hectic time. Until one day she realized that she hadn't had a real conversation with O'Brien in over two weeks. She had *no* idea how the show was really going for him. And, more frightening still, they hadn't made love in at least a week!

Nervous now, and completely unable to concentrate, Taylor managed to rearrange her day so that she would be free to meet Sean at the theater later, as a surprise.

Her last meeting kept her longer than she expected, but she arrived at the theater excited and very much in the mood for the attention they had both been missing.

She entered by the stage door and quickly made her way to the wings. Smiling mischievously, she peered around one of the curtains, only to find that the love scene was being rehearsed by none other than . . .

Trying to remember not to jump to ridiculous conclusions, Taylor felt her face flaming. She still tried to judge the picture from a distance.

She had to admit, O'Brien's behavior seemed to be quite in keeping with that of a director working on a problem. He was reading with his leading lady.

The "lady," however, appeared to have her own problem—that of deciding whether she should be cuddling, groping, or thrusting her spare parts in O'Brien's direction.

Following a simple instinct to protect her investment, Taylor's heels clicked against the wooden stage floor as she proceeded to where the "scene" was about to be in progress.

Two

Five feet six inches could not have been taller.
"Hard to keep your mind on business, isn't it,
Tracy?" Well, she'd never said she was subtle. And
besides, Tracy Dunn was one very "caught-in-the-
act"-looking lady! So she continued, "Or just what
is . . . the business?" Eight years of professional
theater would *not* be wasted here! A defiant stance,
an arching brow, a hint of a sly smile were armor
against the urge to knock Tracy's block off!

O'Brien laughed, appreciating the drama,
displaying a marvelous innocence. A few stammers
from Tracy, and it was all over. But Taylor was still
roiling for a good fight.

She'd never felt real jealousy in her life. Never
had reason to, she told herself. But she managed to
hold it all in until they were home. She crashed
through the front door, made straight for the living room to open the long windows.

After carefully locking the door, O'Brien simply behaved as though nothing had happened, going right to his desk at one end of the room.

Breathing hard, arms crossed on her chest, Taylor waited, for condemnation or apology, but something! Finally, feeling provoked and wanting a little of her own back, Taylor goaded, "I think . . . I'll have to sit in on the casting sessions for *The Run of the Play.* Set you up with a little competition." Soooo nonchalant!

"What?" Sean remarked absently, ruffling through a manuscript.

Wasted!

"Nothing. Not a damned thing!" she said, steely-eyed, before turning and exiting through the hallway, up the stairs, and to the bedroom. She slammed the door.

So there!

So what? He didn't come after her. Of all the nerve!

So she turned on the television . . . *loud,* and waited . . . and fell asleep.

Some time later, she woke to warm, oh, so welcome lips, trailing down her neck, hot and sweet, drugging her senses.

"Oh Tay . . . don't be mad." He nuzzled. Then it registered.

"*What* did you say?!" Taylor asked, now quite wide awake.

"I said, don't be mad. . . ." He stared down into her eyes, bracing himself with his elbows on either side of her, eyes soft.

But hers were absolutely *blazing*!

"*What* did you *call* me?"

Looking puzzled, he shrugged, then said, "Tay."

"You never called me that before in your life!" she accused wildly.

"What difference does it make?" he asked, still puzzled.

"Tay! *Tay!* You sure you don't mean *Tray*, or maybe *Trace*? Getting your women confused, O'Brien?" she bellowed as she threw his stunned weight off her and rolled from the bed.

"You haven't touched me in seven days. When you finally condescend to do so, you have the royal gall to call me by another woman's name. And, of course, *I* shouldn't mind a *bit*! Perhaps you'd like to bring her home to your own bed, where you can be comfortable!" Then the zinger—she was, after all, *very* angry. "Or"—just a small, but perfect, pause—"perhaps you already have?"

"What the hell are you talking about?" His bellow beat hers in any contest. Not that she let *that* stop her.

"What the hell do you think?" She was, by this time, quite beyond rational discussion, striding up and down the bedroom in a fury.

"Stop acting, Taylor, and sit down and talk to me about this nonsense."

Three blows! The big, stupid Black Irishman knew nothing, but nothing, about women, or actresses, or being in love! The greatest taboo when fighting with an actress, as anybody knows, is to accuse her of being theatrical. "*Acting*," indeed! And the very last thing to say to any woman, as anybody knows, is that what she's saying is nonsense. But it always seems to be a man's fastest, most ready excuse. The big schlump! And how could he possibly be so ignorant as to expect reasonable behavior now, when she was half out of her mind with love and jealousy!

However, since she kept these important roots to all knowledge to herself as a form of punishing the man, and in the best interest of her pride, he had no idea of the pit he had just fallen into.

From there on tempers escalated until they both felt betrayed by all the small, hidden resentments of every mentioned slight. Neither was fighting fairly.

Then, unbelievably, O'Brien was packing.

"Don't you dare run out on me! You . . ." She seemed to have run out of names. "You coward!"

"Not a coward," he said wearily. "Just tired." Then, without even the half-filled suitcase, he left.

Crying without end, but not to be outdone, Taylor packed too. Then she waited. But only for ten mindless, eternal hours of the night. She was sure that any minute O'Brien would return. Wouldn't he? But as time passed, she couldn't help remembering another Irishman who'd left her in the night. Then she'd been seven years old and helpless to retaliate. Well, helpless no more.

Leaving no word, not for her mother, or even for O'Malley, she took herself and that beautifully packed suitcase to Reno.

Believing, absolutely, that the best clichés were the oldest clichés, she got the fastest divorce possible and returned to a New York hotel room to lick her wounds.

Two more miserable weeks passed before, finally, weeping to O'Malley, she poured it all out, hoping for some answers.

"First off, luv, you'll come to me." She seemed to have touched on his personal pride, or honor, or something. "A hotel, the very idea!

"Second"—always enumerating—"it's none of my business what goes between you and the

O'Brien. But"—here it came—"for a girl to leave her man"—*her* leave!—"on the slightest provocation"—accent was suddenly quite thick—"well, it t'ain't a thing I can condone atall. Though I'd like to tear his heart out for hurtin' ya." Then, more gently, "But thirdly, I want you to remember, as I do, that you are extrasensitive 'cause of yer da. And the O'Brien, well, he doesn't know about the lovin' and the fightin' together, just the fightin'."

She was getting confused, and suddenly a bit suspicious. "What are you talking about, O'Malley? What do you know that I don't?" She knew the two men were friendly, but she had thought that was as far as it went.

He cleared his throat nervously. "Nothing I should be repeatin', but if it'll help you understand the boy . . ." He drew an unsteady breath and began.

"Sean and I have had a few together, luv, over the years. Uh, and through those years I've pieced together most of the parts. I know *you* know Sean lived with his grandparents from the time he was fifteen." He waited for her nod. "But his parents' car accident happened when he was ten."

"Please, O'Malley," she said, knowing his penchant for a good, long story, and not really wanting to talk about O'Brien at all.

"Ah, yes, luv." He relented. "Well, in the five years between, the boy was shuffled between two sets of relatives, none of the lot with children or love for them. The grands would have taken him first away, but that all of the goody-two-shoes convinced the darlin's they was too old fer a growin' wild thing of a boy. And it seems there was a bit of money involved. But . . . when he ran to them three times in a row, they convinced themselves.

Now, I don't know exactly what went on in detail in those years. But he never talks of that time, and that's a clue. He was hurt, girl, and it left some scars."

"You mean you think that's why he left so easily?" But she wanted answers the poor man didn't have.

"That I don't know, luv. Maybe someday he'll tell you himself."

"Himself" was going to be appearing all too soon. He'd agreed to those conditions, conditionally. Oh, my God . . . they'd not only be seeing each other, they'd be working together! They hadn't even spoken in twelve months. The lawyers had handled it all.

Well, if this was his idea of revenge, it would probably do the trick. Her play, her acting, sabotaged by a master. But—she was embarrassed at the thought—it would almost be worth it to see him again, no matter the cost. But under the same roof? How in heaven was she to get through this one? What will he say? What would she wear?

Then she—stupid, stupid, stupid!—burst into tears. It's just business—he couldn't care less about seeing you, she thought. But she hadn't seen him in a year—a year!—and that made her cry even harder. Then more awful bourbon and sleep, blessed sleep.

She woke to softly diffused light, wondering when she had stumbled to bed. Expecting a headache, she moved slowly and gingerly. A turn, a twist, but, surprise . . . no pain. Instead she seemed to have awakened with that funny, expectant feeling that something wonderful was about to happen. Then she remembered.

"Relax," she told herself, "don't get excited, 'cause it's going to be really horrible."

First thing, she'd have to call O'Malley. Puir, puir man. He'd probably been trying to reach her for hours, just because she had unplugged the phone last night. Oh, well, we all have our cross. She was O'Malley's, she guessed.

O'Brien's coming. O'Brien's coming! No, don't spoil a beautiful day, girl. It's much too early for all that mess. So she started singing at the top of her lungs instead.

An hour, a shower, and two brimming cups of black coffee later, there was a tapping at the front door. A very short amount of tapping before she heard the scratch of a key in the lock. She knew. It could be no one else.

Why did he have to catch her in running shorts and a T-shirt? She wasn't ready yet, not just yet.

When the door opened she was but five feet from it. Poised for flight or welcome, O'Brien couldn't say. He only knew that she looked good, so good. She was wearing one of his old sleeveless white undershirts and thin, yellow nylon running shorts. He wanted to grab her in his arms and never let go, but he stood frozen just inside the door. Possibly more frightened than he had been since he was eleven years old, and trying hard not to show it.

Real people don't look like that, Taylor was thinking, nobody looks like that. And she wanted to cry, even before she'd made it all the way up to the eyes that she was terrified to meet. But there they were. Deep, as blue as the sea, and quite shielded from open expression.

She hoped she didn't look as hungry for the

sight of him as she felt. Her memory hadn't painted him as being as vital, as larger-than-life, as she saw him now. He was wearing an old pair of beaten-up tan cords she remembered, along with a beige crew-neck cotton sweater.

Could she really have forgotten how electric his eyes were? A pulse was beating in one temple as he stood there, unmoving. She could imagine her own heart pounding right out of her breast.

Worlds of time passed. Then came his voice, a little scratchy.

"There was no answer when I called from the airport or from the corner," were his first words to her in a year.

Her lips parted, but no sound came. Then, her hand going to her mouth, she whirled around and ran to the phone. She bent and with slow deliberation plugged the cord into the back, stalling for time. It rang immediately.

"Where the divil have you been, girl?"

"O'Malley." Of course. "How are you?" Ridiculous, but what did she say with *his* eyes on her?

"Stupid question! Worried about you, ye silly baggage? O'Brien's been leavin' a thousand messages with my service, all sayin' he's going right to the house from the airport. Are you hearin' me, luv?"

"Mmmm hmmm."

"So . . . ye've company already?"

"*Mmmm* hmmm."

Only the tiniest of pauses ensued. O'Malley was notorious for his aplomb.

"Well, I'll be leavin' you to it. But call if you need . . . well, you know." Then he was gone. And they were alone.

Pulling together the most self-possession she

could muster, she stood and turned resolutely to face the enemy.

"I'm not the enemy, Red." How did he know what she was thinking?

"Don't call me that!" was all that she snapped, wondering when she had become such a "tough guy."

"I said"—why was he walking toward her?— "I'm not the enemy."

She clenched her jaw to keep it from shaking, and replied, "I never said you were."

He came to a stop just in front of her and lifted her jaw with his knuckles. "We'll just work, Red. It'll be all right. We'll wait to talk until it's time. Okay?" She was a fool, an idiot, but tears spilled anyway.

"Ah, Red, my little Red. I know it's hard." His arms were holding her after so, so long. "It's okay, s'okay," he was whispering into her hair. But she knew what a stupid, stupid horse's behind she was to let this happen.

Pulling away from those too welcome arms, she wondered if he felt as bereft as she at the loss of the embrace. If she could only talk around that mountain lodged in her throat. She cleared her throat, then forced herself to look right into those eyes.

"Sean," she started, but that sounded all wrong already. "O'Brien," she started again. Much better. Then she remembered. There were real reasons she had spent the last year without him. She knew that she harbored a great deal of resentment against him. He had never even called to see if she had lived or died, and now . . .

She refused to believe it was all on the account of one fight—a dilly, but one fight. And those long days and nights were not going to disappear because his touch was still . . . magic.

"I know you're here for business." Her hand signaled him to let her finish, as he started to interrupt. "And that's why I consented to your staying. That's the only reason," she lied. "And we'd better get that clear between us right now." Could he tell she was lying? "I don't want you to think for a moment that I'm inviting you back in my life. Because I'm not, and I won't." She was getting in deeper and deeper. "But there's still this thing between us, so please, please, keep your distance." Got it all out. But what if he laughed at her? On, girl, *on*!

"Uhmm, you can use the bedroom down here." She finally tossed a quick look his way and then, quite rudely, turned before he could respond in any way and grabbed a bag, leading the way. "I didn't know about any of this until yesterday afternoon, and I never thought you'd be here so . . . so soon." Thataway, girl, make every blessed thing you say sound like an idiotic accusation. She never once looked up, so she didn't know she was cutting off any explanations he might have made. "Well, you know where things are, pretty much." Worse and worse! Just shut up, why don't you? . . . Why didn't he say something? Any minute she was going to start pouring sweat. "Well, back to work." Now, *there's* blighted nonchalance for you, definitely worth four years of college! Let me out of here! Well, turn and go, stupid. This is the worst scene you've *ever* been in. So obvious. You blasted out of there like a shot. What do you think he's thinking?

She made it back to the study upstairs in record time, her thoughts still crashing together.

Now she was carrying on another dialogue . . . with herself. "I refuse to be crazy, or to cry, or to sit here and wait for both to happen to me. Run, that's what." So, grabbing her keys and a dollar, she wondered if she could just jump from the fire escape and avoid going downstairs altogether. No, too risky. The cat next door had broken a leg that way. So . . . go on, get it over with.

Oh, yes, she strolled quite beautifully. Stairs done. Uh-oh, the door was still open. So, don't look . . . no problem . . . the front door . . . easy! Now don't slam it . . . aah, free! Now, run like hell!

Thank heaven for the peace of tree-lined streets, junkies, muggers, and dog mess!

In the downstairs bedroom of 22 Bank Street, one Sean O'Brien lay back on the oversized bed looking decidedly smug. Eyes to the ceiling and hands behind his head, he was the picture of a man at ease.

"You're getting to her, old man, you're getting to her!" he congratulated himself aloud.

He knew he had botched things badly a year ago. At the time he had felt driven by the hopelessness that filled him from that fight. Lord, just a fight, how had it managed to get so out of hand? But it had, and it had been as much his fault as hers. And he hadn't taken more than two steps out of their house before he knew he had made a mistake by leaving. But it had been too soon, and there'd been too many things he'd had to sort out first.

He had gotten their BMW out of the garage where they stored it, and driven upstate. Finally stopping in a small town near Woodstock, he had noted the empty gas tank, parked, and begun to

walk. He had started out along the highway, looking for a station, then been enticed by the dark
woods. He'd found a path by moonlight and wan-
dered, thinking about his life with Taylor and his
life before her. At sunrise, he'd known she would
be worried, but he'd thought she'd probably fallen
asleep by then. And, to tell the truth, he hadn't
much minded the idea that she might suffer, just a
bit, for a little longer.

He'd made it back to the West Village at about
noon, believing that he had conquered his dragons
and that Taylor would be overjoyed and quite,
quite repentant when she saw him.

No one. The house was empty, and Taylor's
suitcase was gone, along with her toothbrush. No
note, no message at all. She was just . . . gone.
Well, she was probably cooling off at Rhea's or
O'Malley's. He didn't like the idea that she had
gone to either of them with their business, but
he'd never thought she wouldn't be home as soon
as she'd had time to come to her senses.

He didn't know he'd lost her until a few weeks
later, when the papers came from her lawyers. But
he'd be damned if he would beg to explain. If she
couldn't be bothered, neither could he.

It wasn't until months after that that he
believed she thought it was really over, that she
had really divorced him. How could she let something so special just slip away? He was furious.
Damn her, it was his life too! He stayed angry for a
few months more, then started plotting. And he
was going to do his damnedest to set things right.
He would have to take it slow and easy now,
though, to get everything back in line. But, he
thought ruefully, he might have to start running

again himself, or he might find himself slipping upstairs before too many nights had passed.

She had looked sweet, with her bright hair in that high, swinging braid and her face all fiery-red and surprised to see him. It reminded him of the look she got when he did things to her with his mouth. Hmmm. He could still see the way that T-shirt lay against her skin and the way those shorts rode so high over the back of that tight little . . . whoa, boy . . . slow down! You can't go on like this. Damned uncomfortable!

"Maybe I'll explore a little," he said to himself as he jumped off the bed. The truth was, he was dying to get into her bedroom—to see if he could find, or would find, any incriminating evidence. Because if there was some, he'd rather know about it so he could do a little more plotting. So up he went.

Pushing the door open with one finger, the first thing he saw was the marble fireplace he was already quite familiar with. How many times had they made that old fireplace burn high. Ah, they'd see about that. Hmmm, new colors, new colors, mauves and cremes, with silk irises in the bronze vase. While not exactly feminine, the room did seem devoid of masculine influence.

Well, to work. Bathroom. Rummaging, he tried to be thorough without leaving any obvious sign. No hint here. Swinging the door back open to the bedroom, his face was brushed by the sleeve of the ivory silk robe he had given her on her birthday. Her scent filled his nostrils as he pushed through the clothes hanging in her closet, and he suddenly needed to curtail this operation. The only masculine garment he found was an old terry bathrobe of his. It hadn't been included in the things that had been so meticulously packed and sent to his business manager's address. Somehow, this pleased him. But he did still wonder if she let other men use it.

Finished now, he gave a last glance at the rumpled bed. Tch, tch, he'd better get out of here before he decided to surprise her . . . *really* surprise her.

"I don't care what they say, I know a man can die of this kind of torture—and clothes aren't made for it either!" Still muttering, he made his way back downstairs.

It was four-thirty. Taylor hadn't come back yet. Dammit! She'd better get back before dark. She knew damn well how he worried when she ran around after dark without him. Had she been doing things like that all this long year? He'd tan her little backside! Over to the front window now, he'd just give a look. Ten minutes passed before he finally saw her limping back from the Avenue.

Three

When Taylor came through the front door, Sean was in the middle of *Newsweek*, casually perched on the arm of the couch. But when he looked her up and down, he couldn't help the growl—well, all right, it was a growl—that slipped out.

What the devil was the matter with him, she wondered? She was a little dirty and had skinned one knee and a bit of the leg, but he acted as though she'd done something against the rules. But all she said was, "Puddle," as she started to limp upstairs.

And there the man was, practically breathing down her neck as he followed too close behind her. Well, enough! And she stopped dead in her tracks.

Okay, so it was a dumb thing to do. The behemoth *did* weigh something over two hundred pounds, and he wasn't anticipating any fast moves. Now, she understood the instinct that made him grab her to him, trying to save them both. But she refused to believe that it was instinct that made his hand go right to her breast to do it!

As they began to fall forward, he had gotten a good hold on her and twisted sideways.

She was now perched on one big knee and he still hadn't removed that hand. Breathing hard, he leaned over her.

"You okay?"

"Of course," she answered, and squirmed a bit to get away from that hand. But the friction was lethal, sending sparks down below . . . for both of them, she soon realized, and his arm tightened automatically.

"Stop that, Red!"

"Me?" she squealed indignantly. Then she scrambled furiously for a foothold somewhere between all those legs of his. Standing on the step below him—well, two steps below, he was a big man—with hands on hips, she glared at him like a feisty kitten.

"All through, O'Brien?" Then she sidestepped him, not all light and grace there, and made her way up the rest of the stairs.

He tried, but couldn't control the deep chuckle that escaped him. Lord, it was good to be home! And she was probably right, he thought. Another minute or two and he'd have had her right there on the stairs. Might have been fun. Ah, well, soon enough. She still melted for him, whether she knew it or not. And there was no way he would waste an advantage like that!

In fact, he might as well press the point a little, as long as he had her off-balance.

Following hot on her trail, he found her buried under the sink, in the bathroom cabinet.

"Off that knee!" he ordered, hauling her out easily by the hips, and planted her on the dressing-room stool.

"Will you stop pushing me around!" she blasted, braid swinging wildly. But when she started to get up, his hands clamped her shoulders.

"Stay!" Then he grabbed her chin and said tenderly, "I'll do it."

"Humph!" she said. But stay she did.

He pulled out the first aid kit and started cleansing the "wounds," very much aware of how her eyes followed his every move.

It didn't even sting much until he got to her scraped knee. As she gave a little jerk of surprise, he stilled her with one hand clasping the back of her calf. She could feel each line of each individual finger, she was sure.

Then he did an utterly frightening thing. Eyes fastened to hers, he bent and gave a soft, warm kiss to the place just above the scrape on her knee. She froze. But he said simply, "All better," before rising to his feet, capping bottles, and closing the box.

Looking downward as he put things away, she flexed her leg, feeling for stiffness. The only thing she could feel, however, was every place he had touched her, and the imprint of that child's "make it go away" kiss.

Damn the man! No one else could do this to her. Why him? Blasted Irishman!

O'Brien finished putting things away. As he straightened, he stole a glance at Taylor testing her leg. But she was looking wary again. Deciding that discretion was the better part . . . he made a quiet exit through the bedroom.

Taylor gave a sharp nod of satisfaction to his retreating back. Peace at last!

Closing the door after him, she hesitated, then defiantly locked it. Now she wouldn't be so nervous, would she? Turning to the mirror, she couldn't help but try to see her image as Sean must. Did she look very different to him?

Her skin was damp and flushed from her run, her eyes a bright green. They were still indignant. Her T-shirt outlined her torso, and, even though she was wearing a leotard beneath, neither was proof against the excitement the O'Brien created. Well, that hasn't changed, she thought ruefully.

She turned sideways then, checking her other assets, and decided everything was still in its proper place.

Was he nearly as disturbed as she? she wondered, then watched as a grin appeared. She thought of that little scene on the stairs, his hand on her, and couldn't help but laugh out loud. The stinker!

Good thing she'd never caught him doing that sweet routine with another woman. She'd cut his heart out, she thought, even now.

She didn't stop to question why she was filling the tub, when she had intended to shower. Or, again, why she was using bath oil that cost fifty dollars per bottle.

But she enjoyed that bath.

Taylor was still wandering around her bedroom in her bathrobe with a towel twisted on her head when she heard Sean hollering up at her from downstairs.

Sticking her head around the door, she hollered back, "You call me?"

"Yeah." And from the sounds, she knew he was coming to the stairs. When he appeared, she saw that he had changed into jeans and an old shirt he had never let her throw away. To get away from that shirt she looked him in the eye, but what she saw there threw her right off-balance again. He was as uncertain as she! His expression was noncommittal but all soft, somehow, and he bit his lip on one side.

Nothing he could have said or done could have affected her insides as did that look, and that little-boy stance.

Looking up at her again, he smiled. "You want to go get something to eat, or, uh, you busy?"

Breathe. She had to breathe. "Sure. I'm starving. Did you have anyplace special in mind?" Please, don't let it be one of their old places. Then she said quickly, "A new Spanish place opened up on Fourth."

"Great." He seemed relieved too.

"Give me a few minutes. There's some wine in the fridge if you want it." Her hands were already on her towel.

As she began to get dressed, she couldn't help but think that there was a terrible excitement in this madness. A merry-go-round she wasn't sure she could get off if she wanted to. Not that she thought he controlled it either. No, it seemed more like a script they were both living out. And not knowing the ending scared her to death.

It took her fifteen minutes to dry her hair and change. It was late May, so she just wore a simple white halter dress with low sandals. Of course, it was one he'd never seen before, and she refused to think about how much, she knew, he loved halters. It was hot, that was all.

Then she went downstairs.

"Nice dress," he murmured, but his eyes were on her hair. It was longer now, but so was his. He loved the way it always defied control. Now, as it fluffed around her shoulders, he had to resist the urge to ruffle it lightly.

He put down the wineglass as he stood. "I like what you've done with the couch." She had had it reupholstered in forest-green velvet. "It feels great."

Did he think she had tried to get rid of his influence on the room, she wondered? She said quickly, "I took in O'Malley's cat when he was on vacation. She liked the other upholstery." Good. He smiled. "And I always wanted a black lacquer table."

"I like," he said simply. Then he gestured to the door with one hand on his stomach. "Please, lady, please, there's an earthquake happening here!"

"So, why are we talking about decorating, when there's paella to be had?" she asked lightly, both of them smiling easily now.

On the street he still walked curbside, and touched her elbow whenever too many people passed them or sidewalk cracks became potholes. Why did she find these little things so damned touching?

Soon enough they were in front of the red, home-styled sign of the little restaurant. Down the steps they went, and were quickly seated at a small candlelit table, watching legs go by on Fourth Street. The darkness and the intimacy were very soothing. They had both had enough upheaval for one day.

Taylor found that she didn't have to work at conversation; she was genuinely interested in what he'd been doing in the past year. And her real interest kept him from embarrassment when she asked, "So what about this film, Mr. Director?"

At first he had looked up quickly, as if he were almost suspicious of her motives. But he quickly relaxed, telling her about the project.

He seemed very happy with it—prominent studio, cast, and producers, eight months spent in England filming. No real snags at all until they had to bring it home for editing. Then they found they had to wait eight more months to have the very famous editor they wanted. But they had finished two months ahead of their first schedule and still had to wait on studio approval and distribution bids. So he was at loose ends for the next eight months.

"O'Malley's call was timed perfectly." Then he said the strangest thing. "I'm glad."

And, try as she might, it took a full ten seconds to pull her eyes from those blue ones. Thank heavens the paella arrived.

She couldn't help but wonder, perverse or not, if she would ever have heard from him if the contract hadn't come up. Why was that so depressing. He was here, wasn't he? Hmmmmm, something else to be shelved.

The paella was delicious, but sharing dinner from one pot reminded them both of sharing other dinners out. Dinners when he would eat twice as much as she—finish hers, in fact—have dessert, then complain how full he was and show it not at all.

"How'd your second act work out? Did you settle those timing problems in the dialogue?" She could finally look up at him, knowing that he was now concentrating and all business.

However, this subject was a sore spot. "Just what did you have in mind when you asked O'Malley to be in on *my* rewrites?" She couldn't quite keep the resentment out of her voice. In fact, she didn't keep it out at all.

"Uh-*huh*!" He cleared his throat. "Well, I guess I just want us to be able to work together if problems occur in the script. I thought it was the easiest way."

There was a long pause. Taylor's face and voice were both expressionless. "I don't believe that you had script approval written into the backer's contract." She raised her eyes to send him a look that she hoped would quell all pretensions. "And just what are we talking about here? What problems?" She couldn't help it, it was just too infuriating. "The backers and the producers don't seem to see any problems in my play! Just what problems are you talking about?" He had used that word just once too often. Who was this guy, anyway? Someone who had walked out on her, and heaven only knew what he had up his sleeve now.

But he backed off beautifully. "Baby, there are 'problems' in every production, every script, especially new scripts . . ." But he trailed off as he caught her baleful eye, then renewed his efforts. "You know how I've always had to fight with my authors. *We* never had trouble agreeing on script analysis—I was just protecting my backside, Red."

She had to back off in turn, but that didn't finish it. She knew this would come up again.

He called for the check, and she contemplated,

just for a moment, what might happen if she pulled out her own wallet. She hadn't taken any money from the divorce, but nobody knew your finances like an ex-husband. She had long ago inherited the house. But she was also paying off school loans and had put quite a bit of her own money into her play. She wasn't sure how much he knew about that. *And* Sean O'Brien did quite a bit better than she did. By the time she finished ruminating, they were on their way out, and his hand lightly touched the back of her waist.

Taylor had always been quite sure that, after the basics, it was the little things that made you fall in love with a man. The delicate way O'Brien had of handling her feelings at that little restaurant, from the play to the check, touched her deeply, however much she might wish to fight it.

Maybe he was just working on her, was one thought. But it was quickly dismissed as she felt his hand on her bare back. His thumb just brushed her spine, making instant gooseflesh. Feeling her response, and that small shiver she gave, O'Brien looked down with a twinkle in his eye. Then he pulled her to him, one arm around her shoulders. "Cold?"

He knew damn well she wasn't cold! "A little." One had to save face, after all.

Her scent was killing him. She must have bathed in it, because when he had touched her arm, it came up to him again, teasing his senses.

He smelled of leather, citrus after-shave, and man . . . lovely. They were both quiet on the short walk home.

At the outside staircase to the brownstone, she pulled ahead and reached for her keys, relieved the connection had been broken. Dangerous, dangerous man.

"Good dinner," she said softly. "Thank you."

"Any time," he said, just as softly.

"Well, I'd better get some work done." So she was chicken, but she was *not* going to sit on the couch and neck! "The stereo's in the same place, and the TV too." She gestured toward the cabinet. "And there's more wine, if you want some."

"Thanks, I'll be fine."

"All right, then. See you in the morning." A little too bright, but it was the best she could do.

She woke to the smell of fresh coffee, and O'Brien on the edge of her bed.

"I brought you coffee. Or would you rather sleep?" he asked with a gentle smile.

"Oh, I'm a mess." Hand to her hair, she was very uncomfortable. The nightgown she wore was sheer white, with little capped sleeves that had slipped quite a bit.

"The best kind." His eyes went to her breasts. He couldn't help it, his hand went to her cheek, thumb trailing her neck.

Her eyes closed, but only for a second. Then she moved back against the pillows, freeing herself.

"You said something about coffee?" she asked uneasily. He did have the grace to look sheepish, then handed her a mug.

"I thought I might have a look at the script today. But I didn't want to start without asking you. S'it okay?"

The sweetness of the man! "Of course, but I'd like to put it in order for you first."

"I hate to have you work on a Saturday," he said. "Maybe you'd rather I waited."

She hastily replaced the mug on her bedside table.

"No, no . . ." She threw back the covers to get up. Her nightgown *would* have to be wrapped around her thighs. These things never happened to her except around this wretched man! She jumped out of bed as quickly as she could. Brushing against O'Brien couldn't be helped.

Rosy now, she ran to the bathroom and shut the door, leaving Sean laughing silently behind her.

When Taylor was in the shower, she remembered that she hadn't locked the bathroom door. With a dart of panic, she wondered if she should get out and lock it, and then felt silly. What was he going to do . . . pounce? Well, that *was* possible! Grudgingly she realized how nice it was to have another body living here with her. And Sean O'Brien definitely packed his own brand of excitement.

She thought of her mother, selling real estate in Texas now, and wondered if her father had affected her mother this way.

It was as though she were twice as alive, twice as aware, with Sean around her. She saw things through both their eyes, not just her own. She laughed at jokes she knew he'd like, at people he'd find funny, chose colors—damn that green couch—she knew he favored.

But what now? Just what is it you expect, my girl? You pretend you expect just to do business. But you're not fooling yourself, and it doesn't look like you're fooling O'Brien. He had much too much of the "cat with the cream" look about him. Easy pickin's, lady, he thinks you're easy pickin's.

Well it's not going to be quite as easy as he thinks! If he wants back into this cozy little boudoir, he's going to have to make it very much worthwhile, she thought militantly. But maybe, just maybe, back in her bed was all he wanted "for the duration," as O'Malley said.

Oops! O'Malley! He probably thought they'd murdered each other by now! She hurried then, filled with guilt.

Later, as she made her way downstairs, she heard voices. Sure enough, there was O'Malley. Come to rescue her, no doubt, she thought with a rueful grin, or perhaps just to pick up the pieces and put them in a box.

He and O'Brien were talking together easily when she came into the room. O'Brien noticed her first, but then, he had radar.

"Ah, Red, there you are. Look who dropped by." Yes, he was casual enough, but his eyes were laughing. Sean knew O'Malley too.

Taylor went right to the big, white-maned, anxious-looking man and hugged him. O'Malley was more of a father than friend or agent, made even more so by this past year. He had coddled Taylor when she felt beaten, yelled at her when she wallowed in self-pity, and helped her get her life together again when she was ready. When she had run away to Reno, he had made things right with her producers and allowed her the time to recover before she had to pick up the parts of her own puzzle again. He was a dear, dear man, and she loved him deeply.

" 'Lo, luv. I just dropped by to give you the last of the contracts"—yes, he was checking the two of them out very thoroughly—"and to remind you of Rhea's opening tonight."

"Holy moly, Johnny! In all the—" She'd almost slipped up. "Yeah, I nearly forgot." Her best friend, and she'd all but forgotten!

Sean was eyeing her with sudden interest. "What's this about Rhea's having an opening?" he asked curiously.

Taylor turned to explain, shaking her head at herself. "Rhea finally returned to her old-age-home series, with the help of a little friendly blackmail from Johnny and yours truly." She winked broadly in Sean's direction.

He was rolling his eyes and making faces. He knew what a pushy team the two of them made—he'd been pushed a few times himself. Then he realized what they were talking about.

Rhea had been one of the first to approve heartily of Sean O'Brien, too, he remembered. He hadn't been nervous about meeting her until he looked into those heart-stopping eyes of hers. They measured, questioned, demanded, and accepted him in the space of the introduction. And until he had gained that acceptance, he hadn't even realized that he had wished for it.

By the end of the evening, he was glad Taylor had such a friend. Rhea was a quietly brilliant, multi-talented, sensitive lady with a fierce sense of love and loyalty. Since they'd had their first acting class, Taylor and she had been more sisters than friends, and they had shared much in the years since.

Rhea had started to do a series of photographs in old-age homes. Then a fire had destroyed her apartment, darkroom, files, and all. The loss had devastated Rhea, making her feel as though a part of herself had been vandalized and lost. It took her three years and, apparently, a lot of good-natured bullying to begin all over again. Not that she'd been idle during those years. She was one of the best playwrights around. In fact, Sean had his eye on one of her plays for his next project. Taylor had shown it to him over a year ago and encouraged his interest.

Taylor was feeling terrible that she had almost forgotten such a momentous event. And she was a bit apprehensive about what Rhea would have to say when she heard that Sean was back and why.

Rhea had always liked Sean, but she was never surprised when a man turned rat. She'd had a few rats of her own.

"The Warwick Gallery," O'Malley reminded her. "White Street, eighty-thirty, or she'll wring your neck."

"The details I know," Taylor said. "It's the calendar that escapes me."

But then O'Brien was giving O'Malley one of those male-only, disgustingly knowing looks, and Taylor was sorry she'd said anything. Men could play at being as smug as they liked, but she was damned if she'd supply the ammunition.

O'Brien caught her expression and stage-whispered to O'Malley, "Uh-oh, I feel a freeze coming on."

At that she had to laugh with them. He had read her mind perfectly, disarmingly. Caution here. The man had much more charm than should be legal. And things were getting just a little too cozy.

"Well, Johnny," she said briskly, "we're going to do some work. If you want to stay and have coffee"—she looked at him meaningfully—"you know where it is."

"Ouch!" He held up his hands in mock surrender, looking injured. What a repertoire! "Thrown out with a shovel!" Then, backing toward the door as they guffawed, he pointed his crooked finger at her. "Eight-thirty!" He slammed the door behind him.

Still chuckling, Sean smiled at her easily. "Well," he said at last, "are you going to make good your threat?"

She looked back inquiringly. She couldn't imagine what he was talking about.

"You did say something about work," he said.

She recovered quickly. "So, let's go, boy-o." But as she ushered him upstairs she wished he didn't throw her off-balance with everything he said!

In the study, he looked around at the chaos with a wide grin and pretended joy. Hugging himself dramatically, he threw out, "Home, sweet home!" before she started beating him with a pillow.

Bending meekly under her blows, he cowered, hands over his head. Then, in a sneaky strike, he grabbed her and threw her on the couch, tickling all the way.

"Beast!" she hollered. "Get off me!" She was losing ground. "You weigh a ton!"

At that, he dropped his full weight onto her, then laughed when she "died." Happily settling in now, he watched the act, completely prepared to wait her out.

"Oooh, darling," she moaned. Then, strategically: "Oooh, Michael, my love." With one eye closed, she watched his face change, and gave a mighty shove. He fell to the floor with a satisfying thud and the most beautifully stupid expression!

"Truce! Truce!" she wailed as his eyes narrowed. "I won anyway." But she was still holding him off with her feet.

"Hmmmph," he countered, one eyebrow raised. "I suppose, if we are to work today, that I'll have to let you get away with that." So prim! "But it goes right up on the scoreboard as one I owe you."

She heaved a sigh of relief. "Thanks, massa, I was about to wet my pants!"

"What, again?" he quipped.

Lord, but it was hard to arm yourself against a man who made you laugh so!

After a few more minutes of nonsense, they settled down to work. Taylor organized just ahead of what he read. Half an hour later, he looked up at her, smiling with warm approval. "It's good, babe, really good." From Sean O'Brien, this was not a small accolade. It took Taylor another five minutes of general discussion to be able to look anywhere near his face.

"Now," he said decisively, "I'd like to talk about the second act." She tried to stay casual as he assessed her reaction. Then he went on. "I think it could use a little tightening. I'd like to help. Okay, honey?"

She was wary. Artistic ego is a fragile thing. But the gentleness of his tone and—yes, face it—that "honey" made her much more accessible. "Okay, where?" she responded lightly, and on they went.

Two hours later she was glad she had been receptive. O'Brien had put his finger on each of the weak spots in the second act without rewriting them himself. His questions and ideas were used to inspire her own. And the second act was already the better for it—much, much better.

Stretching happily, she signaled a break, and said, "How 'bout lunch?"

Sean unfolded his long body from the straight-backed chair and stretched, too, hands behind his head. Taylor pretended not to watch as she thought for the thousandth time how tall he was. And she couldn't help but wonder why that very height, something so simple and natural, affected her like an erotic dream.

"Let's take a break out to the real world, Red, and see what we can find to nibble on."

Useless to argue about what he called her, he'd just go on doing what he wanted anyway. "I'd like to see *you* nibble," she answered, then laughed and ran down the stairs as he made like Dracula.

Outside the sun was shining gloriously down on the green-and-white small-townness of Greenwich Village. Pulling her arm through his, O'Brien said, "You know, when I left Surrey, it was still freezing. May! This feels so good." He turned his face up to catch the sun's rays, and smiled. His white teeth worked on her nerves so much that she hooked an ankle around the front of his. He stumbled grandly, dropping her arm as he flew over the sidewalk like the scarecrow from Oz. Taylor walked along with her nose in the air and "I don't know him" stamped all over her. But when he saw that, he came to her and grabbed her by the knees, lifting her high in the air and holding her there.

"Kiss me," he growled, à la Frankenstein.

"No way, Buster Brown." She tossed her head from side to side. "No kisses here."

"Then, no lunch," he answered.

"Lemme down, you big Irish bully!" They were

beginning to attract attention. New Yorkers love a good scene. And, evidently, they didn't think theirs was of a serious nature.

His hands were beginning to pinch at her knees, and she was only prepared to go so far to win an argument.

"Okay, okay, but keep it clean or the deal's off." She eyed him warily.

His eyes were much too triumphant. They locked with hers as he slid her halfway down his body. Holding her at face level, he parodied, "First we start clean, then we gets dirty!"

"Poor Tina Turner!"

"Well," he drew out, "see if you like this." Then he kissed her, her legs still dangling. But she couldn't feel his hands anymore. All she felt was that kiss, filling her senses with things she hadn't felt in much too long. Ah, she remembered his kisses. Her cheeks flamed, and she lost her sense of balance, and that kiss that had started out so sweet was getting way out of hand. She was making protesting noises with her throat, her lips being otherwise occupied, when he finally let her slide down the rest of the way. He ended the kiss by tugging gently on her lower lip with those white teeth, and Taylor had a terrible time keeping it from starting all over again.

Looking around self-consciously, she saw that no one had really stopped, but they were still very much the center of attention on Seventh Avenue. Of course the knowing smiles and indulgent glances didn't bother the O'Brien a bit. *He* was enjoying it thoroughly!

Too thoroughly, she thought to herself, and ground her toes over his. Before he could react, she pushed away from him and walked on, determined to ignore the entire incident, and him.

But, O'Brien being O'Brien, he walked along beside her, mimicking her so outrageously that she had to laugh.

Taylor had always found her sense of humor to be an alarming and exasperating personal trait. It would get her into all kinds of trouble with people who didn't understand why she would burst into laughter; it would embarrass her in quiet moments and at momentous occasions, and it eliminated as friends those who couldn't laugh.

It was also one of the first things that had made Sean O'Brien fall in love with her. And it was his best and greatest weapon against her.

He loved her hair. It was blowing with a will of its own around and about her face. He grabbed one of the longer strands and wrapped it around his finger.

"Just come this way, my pretty." He was the wicked witch of the west and he was leading her onto the patio of the restaurant by that strand of hair.

"Stop that or I'll grab someone's water," she threatened, her hand tugging at his. The waitress thought they were a couple of Village lunatics.

"She thinks we're on drugs!" Taylor hissed at O'Brien as she gave a final yank.

"Let's see if she asks for some," he hissed back.

"Brat!"

He loved *that*!

This was terrible. Things were rushing on so fast. She was having too much fun. She was feeling too much like she did when she first fell in love with the O'Brien. She was feeling too much, period.

After he'd left, she'd felt too much too. And then she had cocooned herself in numbness. It had saved her.

Remember when he left, remember how it hurt, she tutored herself. And remember that he'll leave again, and you'll be all right.

That three-hour lunch went quickly. O'Brien told her stories of his stay in England: the first time he sat down to a traditional English dinner after a hard day on the set, and found that it was baked beans glopped delectably on toast! And the first time he dared go to a pub alone: how no one spoke to him, the stranger, until he started on the dart board. At which time he was suddenly attacked with back-slapping, championship contests, and more ale than he'd seen in his life!

She brought him up to date on New York, mutual friends, the crazy lady who sat on the stoop and tried to sell bad paintings and worse philosophy. And, of course, tales of Johnny O'Malley.

By the time they ran down, Sean had paid three separate bills and tipped two different waiters. Taylor squealed when she saw it was fast getting dark, and raced O'Brien home. When she got to the steps, he was lounging at ease, not a hair out of place—an old trick of his, really. But she raced all the way to the door, inside, and locked him out. She would have left him there a while, but he had glued his finger to the bell and kept yelling in an adolescent falsetto, "Candygram! . . . Telegram! . . . Flowers! . . . Mail-a-boy!"

When she finally controlled herself long enough to be able to open the door, it was to find him eyeing the second-story window.

"I was going to call the cops," she told him, "but I knew once they got hold of you they'd never let you go. And *I* would be out a director and a lot of dough!" Wistfully now: " 'Course I could always sell your car. Ouch!" Her hands went to her backside, rubbing where she'd just been pinched—hard!

He then proceeded to waltz past her on the way to his room. "I don't know about you," he challenged, "but I'm going to make myself *gorgeous* for this big opening I'm going to." And with that he closed his door. Muttering to herself, she made her way up the stairs, a martial light coming to her eye.

Four

"We'll just see how bloody 'gorgeous' the big braggart looks next to this little number!" Taylor was still muttering an hour and a half later in front of her full-length art deco mirror. She was dressed to kill, or be taken.

She was wearing a "sweet little number," a three-hundred-dollar black chiffon outfit that was covered with black and sparkling gold bugle beads. She primped shamelessly as she took in the pants that wrapped tightly around her ankles and the scarflike piece of black satin that twisted over and covered her breasts, leaving her midriff bare. Smooching at herself delightedly in the mirror, she picked up the kimono-shaped see-through jacket and put it on, watching the beads catch the light like a Las Vegas show. Fastening her high-heeled black suede sandals, she gave one last look, checking over her shoulder, grabbed her little black suede clutch, and threw open the door.

With all the panache of a thirties starlet, she made her way down the stairs, swinging everything that would swing.

O'Brien was at the bar making martinis. He might be a six-foot four-inch smart-mouth, but he was a beauty in a tux! And so she told him, believing in giving credit.

Whether it was from her compliment or the dazzling spectacle she made, his eyes were absolutely glowing. Men should *not* be allowed to be born with blue eyes!

"But a tux, O'Brien?" She could afford to look amused, she could afford to look anything, *she* was "bloody gorgeous" tonight!

"I hardly ever get to wear my princely finery," he returned haughtily. He adjusted his cuffs and curled his lip. "Martini, m'dear?"

"Cripes! I'd love it, Charlie!"

"Your hair's sparkling, Red." He did seem preoccupied with something.

"Fairy dew," she answered, and patted the top-knot, with its random rhinestones.

"Mmmm, I always want to pull the pins," he said to himself, moving a bit closer.

One hand clutching her martini, the other in a stop sign, she backed away. "Hands to yourself, or you'll be wearin' an olive!"

He gave an aristocratic shake of his head and sat on the sofa, removing a lilac cushion from behind his back. "My darling, surely you know by now"—he waggled his brows—"that I would *never* deprive you of an entrance!"

"You do what you damn well please." She was muttering again, but he must have heard her, because she could almost hear him shaking with laughter as she crossed to the stereo cabinet.

She put on the radio—she wasn't about to set a mood. There were far too many records in that cabinet that they had shared on evenings much like this one.

Turning from the cabinet, she went to a chair by the window and quietly sipped, only to look up inquiringly. She had felt his eyes upon her. "You look . . . wonderful, Red."

She was stunned. Well, of course she looked wonderful—it had taken her an hour and a half to get ready, hadn't it? But Sean O'Brien was not a man given to compliments, or hesitation for that matter, and he was definitely hesitating.

So she blushed. O'Brien always made her blush.

When he saw it he smiled a very, well, tender smile. Then his eyes seemed to go from her face, down her neck, to the snakelike black satin around her breasts. She knew what he was thinking about by the darkening of his deep blue eyes. Her blush deepened, and his eyes ran down her legs to her very high, high heels. She recrossed her legs uncomfortably under his scrutiny and tried to stare him into shame. But when his eyes met hers, after traveling leisurely back upward (and taking his time about it too), they held only pleasure, and, perhaps, memory.

"Hiya," he said warmly.

"Hiya, yourself," she said back, and the moment hung heavily on the air.

O'Brien looked uneasily at his watch and stood up.

"We'd better move, Red, or be counted amongst the condemned."

Taylor stood in turn and took both glasses to the kitchen. When she turned from the sink he was leaning on the doorjamb behind her, waiting, she supposed, for her to finish. But when she reached the doorway he didn't move to let her pass. She looked up, way up to his eyes. He looked down. Then he said, his voice a little uncertain, "Lovely, Red. That's what I meant to say. You look lovely."

"Oh." Such a bright girl. But she couldn't for the life of her manage to think at all. She could only stare up at him with that stupid expression on her face.

She had always known O'Brien loved her, at least when they were married. But there had been very little sweet talk between them, and she hadn't really missed it. It was almost all she could do to handle the weight of the chemistry between them. She had felt swept off her feet enough. And compliments had never been O'Brien's style. He figured that you knew how things were between you, that more would be gushing, and not in his line.

His kind of compliments were simple and direct. If she looked *really* good, they wouldn't go out to dinner at all, or he would have to have his hand on her somewhere. Or he would tell her with his eyes, or with at most a nod or a "you look great." This was totally beyond her experience of him, and more than a little confusing.

It made a stranger of him.

Finally he held a hand toward her, palm up, and led her to the front hall. "Coat or something?" He looked at her bare midriff, then kept pulling her to the door as she shook her head. Outside, still holding her hand, he locked up with one hand. Silly, really, but endearing nonetheless. He didn't seem to want to let her go.

At the bottom of the steps, he gave a wary look at her high heels, grinned wryly, and pulled her tightly to him, one arm through his.

This was a none-too-subtle reference to the fact that Taylor wasn't terribly secure in high heels on New York City streets. She was fine indoors, but unsteady surfaces and unlikely objects in her path were apt to make her momentarily disappear from view.

However, she still thought it a bit low of him to make reference to what was, after all, a minor personal flaw. So she pretended she had no idea what the big joke was. Naturally.

As they made their way to the Avenue for a cab—Taylor only stumbled once or twice—both of them felt a bit decadent without coats to hide their glitter. But this *was* New York.

At the curb, O'Brien hailed valiantly for a few minutes, until Taylor, with an exasperated sigh, went to stand under a streetlight. It almost became a contest, but she got a taxi too fast.

She tried not to look smug; he tried not to look irritated. The ride was not a chatty one.

They bumped along to SoHo and helped the cabbie locate the gallery. There were some lovely cars lined up and down the warehouse-edged streets. And O'Brien succeeded once again in disarming her. Completely out of character, he stepped over her to open the door when the cab halted after three false stops and reached in to gallantly hand her out. Grinning inwardly and quite flattered, Taylor behaved in the appropriate grande dame fashion.

Mother wanted a man like this for me, she told herself, amused as they made their way casually toward the lights and noise.

Inside, Taylor slipped out of O'Brien's grasp as she spied Rhea in a corner talking to an artistic type.

"Bombs away, Ree!" Hugging her in congratulations, Taylor whispered. "O'Malley *did* tell you the spot I'm in?"

Rhea was chuckling happily. Two inches taller than Taylor, Rhea was a wild ethnic mixture and her own kind of bombshell. She had the figure of a model with cleavage, and long, lovely arms that were constantly moving in theatrical gestures as she spoke. She was a laughing vixen with cow eyes that could stop a truck. She couldn't help that smirk—heaven knew she was practically born with it—but Taylor wasn't at all happy to have it directed at her. "Shall I lie and say I'm not pleased that you two have gotten back together?" she asked. She was wearing a red silk dress, and the color had obviously affected her brain.

"We are *not* together!" Taylor said too loudly, then hissed, "Just where did you get that idea? We're caught in a legal tangle over the play, and he's staying at the house." She ducked her head to hide her eyes. "But that's all!" She threw her head back, "*understand*?" She was bewildered. "I thought Johnny had explained all this by now." Suddenly, looking around at the roomful of people who represented years of friends and acquaintances, she was wary. "And just what do *they* think?" She was getting a bit belligerent now.

But Rhea simply smiled and shrugged, a Gallic gesture and a saving grace, Taylor thought as she made her way to the ladies' room. She needed time to blow off steam before she faced anyone else.

She carried on behind the locked door.

"Damn, damn, damn! And I'll bet O'Brien's just loving it!"

That made her race right back out. As she made her way through the sea of faces, small talk, artistic comments, and knowing looks, she put on her best status quo face and chitchatted with her very best aplomb.

Seeing O'Brien with an old enemy—they were fascinated with Rhea's work—she about-faced and went through the showing on her own. The enemy was an old girlfriend of O'Brien's, and they looked so cozy, Taylor decided to treat herself to their absence.

Determined not to care, she absorbed every bit of the exhibit, and found herself deeply moved and excited by it all.

"Oh, Rhea," she said when she found her friend again. Rhea's eyes just missed her own, so full of thought and feeling. "Rhea!" she said again, compelling attention. She continued with quiet sureness, "I loved the set you started before the fire. I loved the beginnings of this show you let me see. And I think I understand why you needed to have the rest of it to yourself, to let it jell. But Rhea, I'm so touched by these photographs, these pictures. They show such depth and such growth in you. They make such a statement, Ree. I understand now why you had to keep so many to yourself. They cut too deep. And," she added, hugging that tall, incredible woman to her, "I am so proud of you, so very proud."

Tears were in Rhea's eyes, but she denied them. She looked almost pained as she said, "Tay, look. We're all going to go uptown in about half an hour and let the gallery agents run the rest of the show. Please, please, come." Her eyes were big and liquid.

"Couldn't peel me away!" Taylor said with another hug. "This is it, woman, so shine, baby, shine!" And with a last squeeze, they looked at each other and remade promises of friendship and caring that didn't need to be remade. They both knew where they stood. A lot of years and a lot of life had seen to that.

Sean had been nervous once again at the idea of meeting Rhea. She and Taylor had been friends for a very long time, and he wasn't exactly sure of his reception at this affair or any other. But he was a strong fellow, and knew he could handle it, if she wasn't too rough on him.

The moment he caught sight of her, he knew that at least this was going to be all right. Rhea saw him near the door, winked, and then she was hugging Taylor. A few seconds later Taylor had disappeared, and Rhea was moving his way through chattering friends. He had waited patiently as she made her way through the crush. But when she reached him, he grabbed her tightly and squeezed her with a great deal of his considerable might.

He had missed the girl, Taylor's bosom buddy or not. "Mighty fancy, Miz Molly," he teased as he looked her up and down. "Does yo' Daddy know yore out livin' the high life thisaway?"

"You rogue," she accused immediately. "And where the hell have you been? Making silly movies, I hear." And she beamed at him with great affection. " 'Bout time you got home," she admonished. Or was it a warning?

"Oh?" he asked innocently. "Something you want to tell me about?" He had that eyebrow quirked. He was wondering if he should have looked through the bedroom drawers.

"No, not a thing." She smiled, and he knew he wouldn't get a word out of her. But he loved her just the same, maybe more because of it. "Just glad you're home." And then she looked at him with those big, soft brown eyes. Well, he was human, after all, and he wasn't able to believe that anything moving was immune to those eyes. He thanked heaven Taylor didn't have them. But then, she had her own weapons. *Women,* he thought exasperatedly. A poor dope didn't stand a chance!

"So," he said mockingly, "I came to see some Polaroids," then grunted as she punched his stomach.

"Go on," she said. "And if you're not *crazy* about my work, then you *won't* be invited to my party!"

He made his way past a few more old friends, looking for Taylor. And just where had the woman gone to? One minute she was before his eyes, and the next she'd disappeared. What the hell do you do with a woman like that, just follow her around like a pet mongrel begging for scraps? Damned if he would!

It was at just about this time that Amy saw him and pounced. She was a woman he'd gone out with for about six weeks before he first met Taylor, and she had a way of physically attaching herself to a man that made him feel positively claustrophobic, in bed or out of it. Funny, it hadn't really gotten on his nerves before, and she did look good, if a little fluffy.

"Sean!" she cooed before she planted a red-lipgloss kiss on his cheek, "How are you?" She thought she was sultry. "I heard you were back in town to do a play, and is it really one that Taylor wrote? I guess Michael's been rubbing off on her." Where had he heard that name before? "So when are we going to have dinner? Or are you still taken?" Lord, he hated her vocabulary!

"Things are pretty hectic right now, Amy," he hedged as he tried to detach himself. What was she doing here, anyway? Oh, yeah, her father was one of the owners of this gallery.

"Hmmph!" She pouted, then brightened. "Well, have you seen the exhibit? It's positively brilliant, everybody's talking about it!"

"I was just about to start," he said politely. If there was one thing Amy was good at, it was discussing any type of art. It was her only form of civilized conversation. Somehow that little dope changed planes of intelligence, maybe because she'd been weaned on it.

That was when Taylor had started toward him, then switched gears, but he hadn't seen her at all.

He was as impressed as Taylor had been, and happily told Rhea so when he came upon her again a little later.

"You seen Taylor?" he asked her, still trying to detach himself from Amy, while Rhea was trying not to laugh at his predicament.

"Last time I saw Taylor," she answered musingly, "she was having some champagne."

"Champagne?" He was at attention now. They both knew Taylor hated champagne. "Where?" he asked curtly. Amy had finally flitted to someone else, at least for a moment.

He found Taylor by the refreshment table, and her hand *was* gripping a glass of champagne. She was talking to a producer they knew, one he knew had the hots for her. He didn't like the set look on her face at all. So he very casually came up to intrude. Sliding one hand around her waist, he attempted to distract her. She didn't jump, but she did glance. What he said was only, "Hey, Max, how are ya?"

"We were just talking about your new project." At the word "your," Taylor did stiffen, explaining much to Sean. "Jack's a good producer. He'll do a great job." Ah, more answers—sour grapes! Poor Red!

They chatted on about production plans, and Sean relaxed in the business atmosphere. One of his hands was now holding a glass of champagne that Taylor had thrust rather rudely upon him. The other had gotten under her loose jacket to lay lightly on the skin at her waist, asserting his claim.

He hadn't realized his thumb had been moving—instinct, he supposed—until he felt her soft skin turn to gooseflesh and she wiggled uncomfortably against his hand.

"Whoops," he apologized softly, laughing down at her while Max gave them the strangest look. The look she turned back on Sean was quite stern. He shrugged, raised an eyebrow, and the conversation continued.

A few minutes later, Sean's claims having been firmly established, Rhea drifted by long enough to announce, "Rafferty's. We'll meet you there." Max excused himself to collect his friends, and Sean leaned down. "You want to wait, or leave now?"

Taylor moved away from that hand again and answered, "We might have to hitch with one of the limos at this time of night. But I'd rather leave now, if we could." She had decided the chance of awkward questions would lessen with the numbers.

"Right," he responded, and began to maneuver them to the front of the gallery. It wasn't difficult, since people got out of the way of a man his size the same way they got out of the way of a Cadillac on the freeway.

"Oh, *there* you are!" It was Amy, beside a white limousine. Her daddy's, no doubt, thought Taylor waspishly. "Oh, hi, Taylor. You two going uptown to the party?"

My, she was a cute little thing, Taylor thought sarcastically. Why didn't the people who mouthed clichés ever realize how completely they fit them? Or maybe Amy did, and simply had no choice.

Next thing she knew, Sean had accepted a ride uptown. Great. And, as if that wasn't enough, Amy had to keep right on talking. "Oh, and Taylor"— such a "cute" little sly smile—"Michael is sure to be there after his show." Such a "cute" little bonbon, too, to drop into her lap, right in front of O'Brien.

Taylor tried to look vague as O'Brien's eyes narrowed. On the trail, wasn't he?

They squeezed into the back of the limo with six other excited friends of Amy's. Great—two of them recognized both Taylor and O'Brien. They were very flattering, and very sweet, and that was the best that could be said.

After a ten-hour ride—wasn't it?—they finally arrived at Rafferty's. By then, Taylor's smile was plastered on, and O'Brien was looking grim. They both relaxed as soon as they saw Rhea. She ushered them to a big booth where their good friends were already in residence, and miraculously disposed of the white limo gang.

Taylor scooted into the crook of the booth with

O'Brien just behind, making her giggle madly with his imitations of the conversations on the ride uptown. Had it really only taken fifteen minutes?

The next move he made was to squeeze her so close to Marta that she was forced to back up, into his thigh. She jumped at the contact, and he steadied her with a hand on *her* thigh. Under the tablecloth, she tried to pry him loose with one hand, keeping the other on top of the table and doing her best to look casual. But she couldn't budge him and finally gave up, throwing him a venomous glance.

The waitress took their drink order, and Taylor turned her back on Sean, as much as that clamp allowed, and caught up on things with Marta. Thank God she couldn't see Sean's hand under the cloth!

Then his thumb was roving along the outside of her thigh and Taylor lost her embarrassment. Now she was mad.

O'Malley suddenly appeared and pulled up a chair. They talked about the reception Rhea's work was getting and discussed a few of the most special shots. Everybody was having a wonderful time.

That was when Taylor saw her chance for revenge, and she smiled a tiny smile. Without looking his way, she moved her glass, very casually, to the edge of the table, just in front of O'Brien's lap.

Taking a big breath, and holding in her laughter, she pretended to let it teeter. She felt O'Brien's gasp as he reached with both hands to steady it.

That was all she had been waiting for.

As soon as he got hold of her glass, she dropped her right to his lap and grabbed hold. O'Brien choked and reddened. Taylor allowed her smile to widen, just slightly.

It was *lovely*.

Someone was asking her about the play, and as she explained the plot and her plans, O'Brien let one hand fall back under the table. But she was watching him out of the corner of her eye, and as his hand neared hers, she gave him a warning squeeze.

Whether he believed her implied threat or not, O'Brien wasn't taking any chances. So he took a gulp of his drink and tried to relax as much as possible. But that contact was not doing him any good.

Meanwhile, Taylor was having the time of her life. It was turning out to be a *wonderful* party, and she *loved* talking about her play. O'Malley was looking amused at something, but whether it was Sean's reddening complexion or their proximity—she had moved even closer—she didn't know.

Hmm. O'Brien was looking very uncomfortable, and he seemed to be developing a sort of cough.

Then dear little Amy found their table.

She started gushing to O'Brien about the photographs they had both liked the most. " 'Member, Sean?" He was going to say something in response but coughed again instead as Taylor smiled a happy smile.

It was about then that Taylor felt O'Brien slip a hand under her jacket and touch the back of her little satin top. He turned his head and, under cover of the conversation, whispered in her ear.

"You little witch."

She couldn't help it; the giggle escaped her.

"If you don't put that hand someplace safe right this minute you're going to lose a very important part of this outfit." He placed his hand just under the satin.

Well, needless to say, Taylor lost no time obeying *that* threat; she knew O'Brien. But she was still giggling into her drink at odd intervals for the next twenty minutes. By that time they had ordered another round and O'Brien's color was pretty much back to normal. When the drinks arrived, he clicked her glass and mouthed, "Touché," which just set Taylor off again.

Amy was confused. "Will somebody please tell me what the big joke is? Just what *is* going on?"

O'Malley was philosophical. "Don't try to understand, dear girl. We don't even begin to try." Then he asked Amy, a very ambitious little actress, if she would care to meet a certain producer he knew over at the bar. She was delighted. And so was the rest of the table.

Marta was an agent, and a very earthy sort of lady. "Really, Sean," she asked wonderingly, "what on earth did you two ever *talk* about?"

"Well, Marta, my dear"—Sean twinkled back—"we didn't . . . er . . . actually talk." And that was so close to what everyone had been thinking that they were all in an uproar. Taylor laughed as loudly as any of them, but she refused to think about it.

Five

Sean and Taylor left Rafferty's a while later, and began walking hand in hand down the Avenue. The city sparkled brightly around them, with streetlights and starlight vying for attention.

Strolling through a rare, perfect New York summer night, with a "tall, dark, and—okay, okay—handsome" man in a tuxedo was more romance than Taylor could arm herself against. And he *was* gorgeous, from the tip of his shiny black dress shoes to the softer black of his curling hair.

She spent a foolish moment wondering whether she had fallen first for the long, deep creases in his cheeks or those eyes that changed and glinted with every thought. What a sap, huh? But what could she do? The guy got to her.

Taylor looked up sideways at her man. The impulse to tease just a little was strong, and after a short self-debate, she gave in to it. Why should she be all alone in her suffering?

"O'Brien," she began, straight-faced and innocent, "just what *was* it you and Amy did all that time you weren't talking?" She didn't laugh outright at his expression—well, one had to draw the line somewhere—but she had to turn her head away. She didn't often see O'Brien embarrassed, this had been just too rare a chance to pass up. Mmm, interesting color in his face . . .

Finally, conscience struck. "Forgive me, O'Brien." She was still hiding her face. "I was simply not strong enough to resist having another look at that blushing boy I caught a glimpse of tonight." She had begun her little speech with condescension, but spoiled the effect by giggling behind both hands. "Lawdy, lawdy, I jus' loves to see that boy get his comeuppance!" Holding her midriff, she danced away laughing as his hands threatened to strangle her.

Seeing how far she'd gotten from him, he straightened, and his hump, the limp, and blindness in one eye all disappeared in a flash, as if by magic.

"Actually," he began, pulling at his cuffs and clearing his throat noisily, "Amy and I spent very little real time together. If we had, I'm quite sure I would have poisoned her and collected money in payment from everyone she knows." Having second thoughts, he amended with a sly grin, "Well, perhaps just a muzzle—with a time lock."

Then he shot her an odd look, as if measuring her reaction. "Uhmm, she doesn't . . . bother you, does she, honey? I mean . . . you know that you're . . . well . . . the only . . . well, hell!" He scowled and ran his hand roughly through his thick black hair as she looked on with more than mild interest. "Dammit, why am I making such an ass of myself? Get me off this hook, will you, Red?"

"I don't know." She smiled at him tenderly. "I kind of enjoy the sight of your big Irish mouth hanging open."

And his eyes sparkled, sending a hot rush of feeling through her. But that feeling also sent a special warning signal to her brain. The man had been back all of two days! After all the pain, all the lectures she had given herself, she was so much putty in the hands of the O'Brien charm. Uh uh, not so easy. No more cute little sexy games of hide and go seek or button, button.

Sean had been watching her face change, wondering what he had said that would make her go all cold on him like that. Even her skin went to gooseflesh as she gained two inches in height. That was a trouble signal, he knew.

"I'd better get home," she said quietly, looking anywhere but his direction. I, not we, he noted. Well, he certainly wasn't going to tackle this one now. As he went to the street to hail a taxi, he couldn't help the surge of anger he felt. Dammit, why did she have to close up like that? They had been getting along fine, better than fine. Why did she have to spoil it? He wanted to spend the rest of the night making love with her. In fact, that had definitely been the best part of his thoughts all evening. Was she seeing someone else? Was that what this withdrawal was all about?

The ride was tense, and an unhappy silence filled the space between them. She hadn't really thought she would have to face these issues so soon. She just wasn't ready to jump back into the middle of things with O'Brien after so long, in the sack or out.

"We'll talk at home," he announced, breaking the silence. *He* was feeling rejected and, well, aroused, and not exactly at his most patient.

"Fine." My, weren't they civilized? Taylor mused. What in the world was the matter with him, anyway? She was the one being asked to take all the chances. And just what would happen to her when his film was ready for editing? He'd go trooping happily off to Hollywood, and she'd be left with wonderful memories of her fling with her ex. Super.

As Taylor was banking her fires of indignation, O'Brien was filling with his own fine slow rage.

Finally they were home. Taylor opened the street side door and got out—an illegal move and a rude one—leaving O'Brien to pay the lecturing cabbie.

Inside she faced him, both of them grim.

"Let's sit down, Red," he began. It was more an order than a question. She sat.

"Who's Michael?"

He had anticipated any look but the one she wore. It was as if he were from another planet and hadn't spoken her language.

"Amy!" She laughed shortly.

"Amy?" he asked. He really thought he was being remarkably patient.

Taylor was shaking her head in exasperation. "Amy is infatuated with Michael, and we've been working together on and off on a project of his. Amy's just jealous."

Sean's brow was thunderous. "Of what?"

Taylor just looked at him, then burst into

laughter. "Well, O'Brien, it *is* a well-kept secret, and Amy doesn't quite believe it anyway, but Michael is only interested in other men." She let the bombshell drop, chuckling to herself about the damage that little dip Amy could do without even trying.

"Then, what happened out there on the street?" he demanded.

It was a question Taylor was not really ready to answer, but neither was she going to pretend she didn't know what he meant. So she did the best she could. "This is all just a little soon for me, O'Brien. I can't make these transitions that fast. And I don't want to. . . . You mind?"

He gave a shrug that was nowhere near easy-going. "You're entitled." Then they were both still for all of a minute and a half before O'Brien took a great breath and wiped the imaginary sweat from his brow. "Whew!"

Taylor grinned, nodded once, and returned, "Whew!" Then, before she could get into more trouble, she stood up and made for the stairs.

"Time for bed." And there was no doubt she meant "alone."

On the second stair, still with her back to him, she finally gave in. "O'Brien?"

"Mmmm hmm?"

She hesitated, and, keeping her back to him, said, "It's good to see you."

"You, too, Red," he answered simply.

She paused, head down, for a millisecond, then made her way up the stairs.

Over the next few weeks, they maintained an almost businesslike distance during the rewrites. No more casual touches or references to past or future. They concentrated on getting the play in shape for the scheduled rehearsal date. They both knew how to concentrate when it came to meeting a deadline.

Mornings they would write, afternoons they held casting sessions. And the only major disagreements they had were both in the same day, one in the morning, one in the afternoon.

In the morning they had argued over the ending of the play. Taylor was convinced the comedy should finish with the romantic leads at odds and alone, but better prepared for their next relationships. O'Brien disagreed, absolutely. Each discussion ended with the unspoken ultimatum: "I'm the writer"-"I'm the director." They were still battling when it was time to leave for the theater and afternoon auditions.

Until that day, they had, luckily, hardly disagreed about casting. That is, until they began to cast the male lead.

One after another the men came onstage. Taylor read with them all. None of them struck sparks, until one large, rawboned young actor read. He was a football-hero type, fresh from the Midwest and a previous law career. He *did* have something, but Taylor didn't feel that it was enough to make up for his lack of professional experience. Besides, she already had in mind a brilliant actor she had seen in a couple of Off-Off Broadway productions.

After the auditions, the producer, stage manager, Sean, and Taylor sat around the long prop table and rehashed them. Sean and Taylor made their feelings known, both of them still raw from the morning. They seemed to be covering the same ground, going round and round in circles, until finally Taylor stood up, slamming her script on the table in frustration.

"Dammit, O'Brien!" Her face was flushed with anger. "I swear you're just getting back at me because I don't want a damned clichéd happy ending! We don't have the time to bring this kid along, and I know Jackson's available, so *why* are you fighting me?"

But O'Brien had a temper of his own. Calmly, deliberately, he stood up too, placing his knuckles on the table and leaning forward to glare into her face. "I am 'fighting' you, you spoiled little witch, to get the best actor, and, incidentally, the best ending for your damned play! *Which*, I believe, should be the first consideration here, not temperament. If I wanted to get back at you, I know a few easier ways."

He couldn't mean . . . did everyone else realize what he was talking about? she wondered.

"Now"—he seemed to calm suddenly, knowing he'd gone too far—"I suggest we break for the day and talk about this tomorrow."

She struggled to control her furious breathing. She would not give him the satisfaction of another outburst. Contrary to what he would like to believe, she was a professional. So she threw back her shoulders, nodded silently, but regally, and sat down to collect her odds and ends, her composure somewhere amongst them. The other two men made their farewells very short. And soon Taylor and O'Brien were left facing each other alone across the wide table.

Silence reigned. Taylor was so angry that she could hear the pounding of her own heart above it.

O'Brien sat across from her, feeling very much ashamed of his tactics, but still very sure of his

71

stand. The other thing he was sure of was that he was about to receive a much-deserved tongue-lashing. He didn't have long to wait.

"If this is a sample of how I may trust you, O'Brien, I'm not sure I care to see the whole pie. But, I warn you, belittling me doesn't shine your armor in anyone's eyes but your own. And now"— she stood and turned from the table—"if you don't mind, I believe we're finished with most of the rewriting. I think it would be much better for both of us if you were to stay somewhere else. The house is a little confining."

But there he was before her, his eyes shining with regret, his arms reaching for her. And before she could think to step back, she was enclosed in those big arms.

"Oh, love, I know I'm an absolute sod. I can't believe the things that I said to you. I have no excuse except that it's been driving me crazy, having you so near, yet not having you at all. But if it's any consolation to you, those two know you and your work and respect you too much to be affected by what I might say in a temper."

"But," she started, her face against his shoulder, trying hard to resist him, "you did say those things." Then she lifted her face and glared into his eyes. "Damn you, O'Brien! I have as much right to my educated opinion as you do, without the benefit or penalty of your low blows." He winced, but he took his medicine. He would have felt the same.

His eyes were deep and sad and pleading as he lifted one brow, his arms loose now around her. "You're right, Red." His stare was intent. "But I'm not going. You can try to get me thrown out if you want, but I'm not going."

Whether she wanted to or not, part of her was

forgiving him. She fínally gave in. "All right. But either we play by the rules or nothing . . . agreed?"

"That doesn't mean we can't fight, does it?" he asked mischievously.

"Heaven forbid!" She grinned back.

"A bargain, then, as long as we seal it in the usual manner." He really was an evil man!

"If we *have* to." She sighed.

"Ahhh, the good stuff!" he murmured just before he bent to kiss her. It was a lovely, long apology, and by its end she really had forgiven him. But he had more atonement due. "I truly am sorry, Red," he whispered against her ear, kissing between words. "I can't excuse the things I said in front of other people. I really am ashamed. I don't know how I could hurt you so."

She couldn't think of a thing to say. So it was a good thing he continued. "How's about you let me make it up to you with dinner at a fantastically expensive restaurant and a play?"

"Now, that's the kind of apology I like!" She smiled, pulling gently away from him. "Of course, the next time you'll have to up the ante, so don't outdo yourself." As she began to collect her script and purse from the table, she lectured herself against the urge she'd had to stay in his arms. His eyes followed her, and she wished she couldn't feel them on her.

"Will you do me a favor in return?" His voice was soft, compelling. She allowed herself to look at him. "Will you wear what you had on at Rhea's opening? I want another chance to wear that stiff shirt."

Why such a simple request would make her blush, she had no idea, but she could feel the heat in her cheeks. Feeling awkward and shy, she wouldn't face him, but she did try to sound casual as she turned away and said, "Sure."

On the way home they talked about the supporting cast, pro and con, nearing decisions. Suddenly Taylor turned to Sean with a light in her eye, the only lively thing in the rush-hour traffic downtown.

"If you really want to apologize, O'Brien, take me to see *Cakewalk*. You can see Fen Jackson firsthand, and I hear it's a very good play."

"Fair enough, but I still have a feeling about Blackman. That kid is just exactly what I see for Jack. But"—he threw out his hands palm up in front of him—"never let it be said that I'm a close-minded, pigheaded Irish bum."

Now, where had she heard that said before? Oh, that's right, *she*'d said it, four or five hundred times.

"I'd be pleased as punch to go see *Cakewalk* with you, my love."

Looking out the window, she muttered as if to no one, "Yeah, maybe a punch."

His loud guffaw surprised the cab driver and pleased Taylor greatly. But she was tired of misgivings and worry and fear. She wanted to feel alive again. So she stilled the voices in her head—told them to go to Hades, in fact—and turned to face Sean and a wonderful evening. Beyond that, she wouldn't think.

Later, as she was dressing, she wondered why he wanted her to wear this outfit, but she couldn't fathom it. So she wore her hair exactly the way she had before and strapped on those high, high heels. Then, just for luck, she sashayed down the stairs just the way she had before, and found O'Brien waiting for her once more with a pitcher of martinis.

"Ah, the twilight zone," she remarked, taking the glass he handed her.

"No, just a rewrite," Sean returned smugly. Now she thought she understood. Control was important to a director. She wouldn't have thought he would be so obvious, though. Somehow she found it oddly touching.

"Play first, dinner later," Sean announced, raising his glass. "To making up."

"Making up," she echoed, clinking glasses, grinning on one side in mockery. Well, he *was* laying it on a bit thick. "O'Brien, don't you know anything? The seduction doesn't happen until *after* you've plied me with food and wine."

"Oops, forgot." Nobody could look sillier than that big Irishman making faces.

"Well, if I can't have you now, I'm certainly not going to risk being late for the curtain. So let's hit the road." He grabbed her barely tasted drink, set it down, then grabbed her hand and dragged her to the door. He locked up, then grabbed her hand again, forcing her into a trot beside him.

"O'Brien!" she cried, trying desperately to keep her balance as he pulled her along. Then it happened, just like a thousand other times before. Down she went. It was *his* fault, his and the bloody race he was running! Sitting on the sidewalk, she looked up at him accusingly. He knew damned well she could barely walk in high heels, much less run relays. "Satisfied?" she asked from down below, the reproach shining from her eyes.

"Lord, I'm sorry, Red." He bent to his knees and checked her legs. "I wasn't thinking." Never would he tell her to give up her heels, though every time she wore them, he crossed his fingers that she wouldn't break her leg.

"Did you hurt anything, dear girl?" His fingers were still moving over her ankles, sending shivers up her legs to center in the base of her spine. "You think you can stand?" he asked as he held out his hand, quite unable to disguise his amusement.

"Yes," she said, clenching her jaw. "I feel quite able to stand—and crush insteps, if need be." She ignored his mirth. "Very romantic, O'Brien." She enjoyed her sarcasm as much as he enjoyed the picture she made.

Finally she sighed in exasperation. *"Get a cab, O'Brien!"*

And that he did.

The play *was* excellent, and so was Jackson, O'Brien conceded. But he wasn't the right type for Jack. Blackman was. Jack wasn't an aesthetic ethnic type, he was a bewildered all-American, unable to cope with the big city and a demanding personal relationship. This guy *was* brilliant, but that didn't work in his favor. Too much angst. But to convince Taylor . . .

Oddly enough, Taylor was having the same revelation. She really *hated* it when Sean was right. She wasn't, however, so ungenerous that she would disagree with him for the sake of argument, though sometimes she felt like it. So, while the third act of the play wound its way around the stage, she tried to think of a gracious way of conceding defeat.

After some time, she decided that she would manage somehow over dinner, though it would spoil the expensive meal she had every intention of ordering. Satisfied, she turned her attention back to the performance.

Each watching the other unobtrusively, they applauded with enthusiasm.

"Excellent show," he said.

"Quite," she returned. The subtext was indescribable. They were on to each other.

They returned their attention to the stage for a few curtain calls, then maneuvered their way backstage. It was quite a crush, but they made their way through slowly until they found Fen Jackson.

Sean, true to form, looked the young, tortured-looking actor right in the eye and said, "You are a wonderful, exciting actor and I would very much like the chance to work with you in the future, on just the right project." He did send a sideways glance toward Taylor. "I think I might know of a film script, if you're interested."

This was Fen Jackson's first real success, and Sean O'Brien was a director he would have killed to work with. Heaven was in his lap.

"Mr. O'Brien," he said with a directness that had to be admired, "I am very interested in any script you would choose to direct. I'm a great admirer of yours and your wife's." He smiled hastily at Taylor. If it was only flattery, Taylor thought, he was really very good at it. But that hardly mattered in the final analysis. His talent did.

O'Brien had one of his cards out, and was scribbling quickly on the back. "This is our home phone. We'll talk over dinner one night soon." His look asked for agreement, which Fen was quick to give, and with a great deal of energy.

"Good show," O'Brien said finally as he

nodded and ushered Taylor back through the crowd. Fen Jackson was wearing only the second smile many people had ever seen on him off a stage, and it went ear to ear.

Six

The little French restaurant O'Brien had chosen was dark and intimate, with red velvet, chandeliers, and secluded candlelit booths set with sparkling crystal. Taylor tallied the price for this apology, and counted it among his better efforts. Not to mention her own.

After a bit of wine, they were served the appetizers. It was all quite lovely, but Taylor was ever impatient.

"So were you waiting until after the sole to start working on me? Or were you hoping that I'd admit you were right all on my own?"

Who would have thought she could still surprise him? His hand stopped midway to his glass, and he looked up with a smile. "Right to the bone of the thing, as usual, me love." He laughed and picked up his glass. "To my girl's true vision. It helps cut all the arguments down to half the usual time."

With someone else, Taylor would have been wary of sarcasm, but O'Brien was a man with unusual taste. He certainly had an unusual sense of humor. She had no fear that his mockery covered anything other than admiration. So she shrugged, looked smug, and said, "Talent."

"You know"—he switched tactics—"I do want to work with Fen Jackson—you were right about him. But, after seeing him onstage, we both know he's not Jack." He looked for agreement in her eyes, which she gave freely. "I only need to know," he continued, "if you're willing to take a chance on the Blackman boy?"

Taylor sighed and shrugged. "I do trust your judgment, O'Brien, but there are a lot of factors involved here. I'm not sure we can afford a relative amateur, though I do believe he is talented. But I have to be practical." He motioned her on with a nod. "First there's a time consideration. Who's going to work with him and when? You know as well as I do that he'll need special attention. Then, of course, there's the gamble. He might not come through. Where does that leave my play?" He only looked thoughtful and waited for her to continue. "Well, I do have a great deal at stake here, O'Brien." Why did he make her feel she was refusing an artistic challenge by being practical? Why didn't he say something?

Finally he raised his big head. "Red . . ." His look went right through her. "We both know that you could never refuse a challenge." He let that sink in for just a second. "And we both know you made up your mind the moment you saw Jackson walk onstage." She flushed so easily. And what had ever made her think O'Brien didn't fight dirty? "I know you want to panic. But I'm here, love. Did you think I don't care, or that I'm not aware of the problems or the gamble? You know as well as I, so I won't lecture you on the nature of the theater. We don't do it to make money, do we?" Then he smiled a sad sort of smile and took the leap. "Or did you perhaps think I might *try* to hurt your play?"

Thank God she couldn't get any redder and confirm his idea of her doubts! Oh, he'd said it all, damn him! And he was right, of course. It was really too infuriating!

She shook her head, compressing her lips. "If you keep being so damned reasonable and so *bloody* right, I swear I'm going to bash you with a candlestick! Really, O'Brien, I just might stick you in your sleep!" With that, O'Brien began to choke over the bite of Coquilles St. Jacques he had taken, *really* choke!

She rose and rounded the table, making a fist. She pounded on the center of his back three or four times. "Please be okay, O'Brien, my Heimlich maneuver is really rusty." This set off another spate of coughing. "Can you swallow a bit of water?" she asked his red face. "I really can eject whatever it is, if you want." He signaled no frantically with his head.

Finally his coughing calmed. He glared up at her accusingly with watery eyes. "You did that on purpose," he grumbled hoarsely.

"Well." She smiled back at him nastily. "I *have* been working on my telekinesis. Of course," she continued as she returned to her place, then rubbed one ankle against his, "it never works quite as well as the real thing."

His reflexes were incredible. As soon as he felt

her ankle, he pinned it with his own against the booth. "No games tonight, Red. It's been too long . . . much too long."

She stared into his eyes. They looked so dark in the candlelight. She didn't know what she read there, but somehow it pleased and excited her. She felt like she wanted to shiver with the suspense and tension of the moment, but she couldn't take her eyes from his until she had answered that look.

They both started at the sounds the waiter made near them. The tension broken, Taylor waited until they had been served before she raised her eyebrows and inquired with a small grin, "Extra service charge for discretion, O'Brien?"

But he merely grumbled something beneath his breath and began to mutilate the delicate fish on his plate.

After a few bites, his composure returned, and they began to talk easily again about new music and openings around town. By the time they got to the coffee stage, Taylor was itching to go. This setting was just too intimate. It colored every bit of conversation with innuendo.

O'Brien was looking mighty tense too. And suddenly he said, "What d'ya say we blow this joint?" Taylor smiled in relief and nodded.

The presenting of the check was a major production they both enjoyed thoroughly as they watched the *maître d'* perform his whole routine, complete with flourishing hand gestures. They exited with answering pomp—that is, until they reached the very last doorway. At that point O'Brien bent slightly, made swimming motions with his long arms, and ushered Taylor to the street with a final "Moddum." Then he straightened, grabbed Taylor's arm before she fell, and asked, "What the hell country do you think they go to to learn that accent? It sounds like they all train with a hard-boiled egg in their throats."

They laughed for nearly three blocks, each trying to outdo the other's imitations.

The third block was near the end of Central Park. For some reason, there was not a soul to be seen. O'Brien felt he had waited long enough. Under the shadows of a big leafy tree, he stopped mid-stride and turned to Taylor.

"Come 'ere, you," he ordered huskily. But he didn't wait for an answer. He pulled her to him with a grand sweep her thin spiked heels couldn't possibly have withstood, and gathered her up tightly against him.

Taylor had seen this coming, and had been determined to resist—at least a *little*—but she never even had a chance.

After all, O'Brien was no mere "puller and grabber." He was a painter of pictures.

Burying his face in her knotted curls, he murmured softly, "God . . . just the way you *feel* against me!"

Slowly, hands riding her bare waist, he nuzzled her left temple, letting his lips slide down to just beside her eye. Brushing her skin alive with every word, he sighed. "You look so beautiful in the moonlight. I can remember everything . . . everything." And so could she, as her heart began to give her away with its pounding. He must have felt it, too, because his hand moved to rest there, just above her breast, and he pressed lightly.

"Did I do that?" he whispered over her ear just before he shaped it with his tongue. She had no knees! What had he done to her knees?

Now he was at the curve of her cheekbone.

Hurry, hurry, please, hurry! And, at last, her lips. Yes, there. But lightly, so lightly did he brush each corner, following with his tongue, just tasting. Her mouth needed his desperately, and she finally found him.

Her arms were wrapped around his neck, her hands in his hair, before she even wondered how they had gotten there. His arms were crushing her ribs, but she didn't care. She could feel every line of his strong warm body. She could feel him hard against her. With woman's instinct, she pressed back, defining his shape and desire. His arms tightened even more as he groaned into her mouth. Their kiss deepened.

"Mmmm." She didn't know if that was O'Brien or herself, but it mattered not at all. His hands were squeezing her buttocks, kneading them sensuously. She couldn't get enough air. But, oh, that felt so good, so very good! His mouth was like warm honey, and as it moved so sweetly over hers, colors rained behind her eyes.

At some moment in time, it vaguely occurred to her that she wasn't resisting, but this was very much more important.

Lord, just to feel these feelings that she hadn't experienced in so long, to give in to this lovely swelling haze of emotion. It defied her sense of reason and didn't last through memory, but it was here now, and very, very welcome.

His hands had moved to her bare back, still kneading, as he kissed the curve of her neck near one shoulder. Her hands moved to slip under his jacket and caress his back. She wanted to be closer, much closer.

With his low growl, she nearly came unglued. She remembered that sound quite well. It usually presaged the moment just before O'Brien lost his "civilized man" veneer. The images that sound evoked were a little too exciting for New York City streets, and she knew she'd better get herself back in hand. But then he was kissing her again.

Taylor finally managed to throw her head back and away from that kiss. How she wished they were home! Backing away, as far as his arms would allow, she could see that O'Brien's eyes were glazed and seeking. That look sent an erotic jolt right through her.

Eyes on his, head moving from side to side, she said, "Get me home, O'Brien." Seeing his eyes change, begin to focus, she leaned back into him, her forehead pushing into his chest.

Pressed against him, her head lifted with each deep breath he took. Ha! They were all deep, and so were hers! Finally, after a moment, he gave her a rib-crushing squeeze, apologized at her startled cry, and stepped away.

He went as far as the curb before he stopped, his back still to her, head bent. After a few seconds he shook his head as if to clear it. Then, when he turned his face and she saw his profile, he shook *her* to the core. His expression was as defenseless as a babe's. It was one she had never seen on him before. She wondered if he knew she could see it now.

She found it difficult indeed to imagine her love as vulnerable or needy. It was one of the reasons she rarely called him anything but "O'Brien." He was always "football-buddy" tough.

O'Brien was brilliant at work, wild in his play, quick in the shower, slow in his loving, and . . . and he made her laugh. He also made her feel beautiful and special in every deliberate way a man could. But . . .

Though his lovemaking had always been tender and expert and satisfying, somehow she had always had a sneaking suspicion that there was more to be had. As if he were withholding something, not in his giving, but more in what he took from her. He wanted her, she knew, but he had never seemed to really need her.

Now, *this* look, this was vulnerable and wanting and needy and alone in a way she had never seen. And she had never loved him more.

Well, she supposed, such was the nature of woman, or, at least, this contrary woman.

At that moment Taylor realized that she would do anything she had to to get him back. This man *belonged* to her. And whatever it took—time, wiles, or compromise—*that* she would give. O'Brien she would have!

But this was a personal revelation, one that she was not yet ready to share with her love. So when he finally looked back at her, a bit rueful, and said, "Cab, hmmm?" she just nodded, taking in every bit of his devastating length, tough features and bottomless eyes.

This woman had every intention of taking *this* man home to her bed as quickly as possible and giving him a night of utterly exhausting pleasure! She tamped down her own excitement as much as she could—it *had* been a year, after all!—and watched him as he hailed a cab and held the door for her.

Sure of her purpose, Taylor planted herself in that checker cab with all the demure, dignified fragility of Olivia de Havilland in *Gone With The*

Wind, leaving O'Brien to spend the ride back downtown collecting himself.

He wanted her. More than he had ever wanted a woman in his life. But he wanted more than the physical pleasure they had always shared. He wanted her in his life, as his partner, in a way that he had never really experienced, although they had been married. He had never realized just what that could mean before. They had loved and shared their lives, yes. But he had never felt this close to Taylor, this needy of her company and care. He wondered if she felt it too.

But, whether she did or not, he would make her feel it. He knew, of course, that she wanted him. But she was going to want him and need him so much by the time he was through, that he wouldn't be the only one to feel this thing. Yes, she would be his, and this time he would know what he had.

Looking at him across the seat, Taylor found that he had stretched his legs out diagonally, his feet almost touching her own. Moving her eyes upward, she saw that his were closed, his head leaning back against the seat. His jacket lay open, hands stuffed somehow into his pants pockets, and the picture made Taylor want nothing so much as to cradle him to her and never let go.

This ride was taking forever.

Where was this guy taking them, anyway? she wondered in annoyance. New Jersey? Finally they were past the warehouses and turning across town. Streets became shorter, more narrow. Taylor was filled with the same excitement she always felt with O'Brien.

"Here!" she croaked out at the same time that Sean barked, "Stop! This one."

No, they weren't anxious. . . .

He was still fumbling with his wallet long after Taylor had thrust a ten at the bored driver. Well, she'd had it out since Forty-second Street.

"Keep it," she said as she got out curbside, keys in hand. Then she looked at O'Brien. Her big, beautiful mountain with a cat's grace was stumbling over his own feet as he maneuvered out of the cab. The cab driver would think him drunk, but she knew better.

She wasn't even aware of the wide smile she wore as she thought that O'Brien must have been thinking ahead too. Only, he must have been a mite further along in his thoughts than she was. Casually, trying to recover his dignity, he finally looked up.

"Get that look off your face before I cream you!" he muttered.

"Uh-*uh*, O'Brien," she said, shaking her head, setting him up for the kill. "Ye really think ye're able, ye puir old boy?" she threw at him, arms akimbo. Then she turned and darted up the steps as he raised his arms to the sky in supplication and asked the stars why in the world he had ever wanted to marry an actress.

He let her run on ahead of him for the sheer pleasure of watching her, then ran up behind in case she decided to lock him out again. He wasn't really worried, though. His little fire-eater never pulled the same stunt twice.

Once inside, he closed the door, secured the lock, shrugged off his shoes and jacket, and headed for the stairs in a few smooth motions. He seemed to have gotten his coordination back, anyway.

Though he could take his time getting to her

now that they were home, his blood was racing. He knew that he would only be able to slow down when he had her in front of him.

Upstairs Taylor quickly unfastened her shoes and, panting slightly, slipped behind the bedroom door like a poor man's Mata Hari, waiting to pounce. There she stood straighter, her heart pounding wildly, oddly aware of every inch of her skin.

The bedroom was dark, and his giant frame threw a giant shadow across the floor past the doorway.

"Red?" he ventured.

She thought later that he must have felt her presence in the very air around him. For, just as she readied herself to shove the door against him, he pinned her to the wall with the same move reversed. Surprise, more than the force of the door, sent the breath from her. But she was still unable to breathe as he pulled the door away.

Ungluing herself from the wall, Taylor tried to walk away as if nothing had happened, but O'Brien was having none of it. Before she had gone two steps, he had grabbed her by the shoulders and turned her to him. With one quick pass, he had pushed the silk of her kimono from her shoulders and pulled her to him by the rope of its weight at her elbows.

"Woman, if you want something to eat or drink, you had better tell me now," warned the face bending so near to hers. "Because I won't be letting you an inch from that bed for weeks." Then he kissed her hungrily. "Maybe months," he finished as he let the silk slide whisperingly to the floor. "Never mind," he went on in a gruff voice, "I can't take any more waiting for you." And he held her face between his two big hands for just a moment before his mouth sank down upon hers.

Desire crashed upon her, breaking her into tiny disjointed pieces. Pictures of the two of them making love flashed behind her eyes. So many times, so many ways, but always there was *this* feeling, *this* magic.

She couldn't have stopped what was happening right now for earthquake, fire, or flood. For they were nothing compared to what was going on inside her.

O'Brien wasn't playing anymore. His need for her was deadly serious. Heaven forbid she should pull away from him now. He wasn't at all sure he could stop.

At this moment this woman, her love, were as important to his existence as oxygen. And the sheer pleasure of holding her, kissing her, was overwhelming.

But very soon it wasn't enough. His hands splayed over her sides, fingers extended. They moved excitingly in tiny circles over her ribs, her waist, her back, forcing a moan from her mouth, where he echoed the rhythm with his tongue. The breath whooshed from her lungs, and she gasped deeply, beginning to tremble.

At last he found the hook in the center of her back and pulled her tightly to him as it fell away. His thumbs lightly followed the line of where the satin top had lain against her, then moved under the material pinned between them. Slowly he replaced the material with the velvet of his hands, caressing her, feeling her nipples harden even more. Her special scent filled his nostrils.

"The night of Rhea's opening I had a dream about you. This is what you were wearing." Suddenly he moved away from her with a low sound of impatience, leaving her to look around blindly, wanting him back.

But he had only released her to grab her up in his arms and take the four short steps to the edge of the bed. Once there, he lowered her and went to his knees on the floor beside her. Their eyes met as his arms fell away, both of them measuring their effect on the other.

Her eyes glowed softly in the dim light from the hallway. His seemed to glitter. She couldn't take her eyes from his mouth. It was parted slightly, and she could all but feel the shape of it against her own. One of her fingers went up to trace it. His mouth opened to capture that finger.

Her lips were parted, too, soft and full-looking from his kiss. He wanted another. He nibbled on that finger until she replaced it with her mouth. But all he did then was lightly cover her lips as he covered her breasts once more with his large hands. Then, as his thumbs found her nipples, his tongue plunged deeply, hungrily, and met her own. With a sigh of satisfaction, her arms went up around his broad shoulders, feeling his heat through the crisp material of his shirt. Her hands went to the open vee at his throat, and she laughed huskily as she slipped each buttonhole easily around the small pieces of onyx.

"You've been practicing!" he accused.

"I have my dreams too." She laughed back, which he answered with a wicked look before he bent to nip at the tip of one breast, then returned to kiss it. His voice deepened as he said, "Shall we work on your dream or mine?"

But Taylor found that the question had flown from her mind as Sean suckled one breast. He was sending darts racing through her to end some-place low in her stomach. As he moved to her other breast, he ran one hand slowly over her silk trousers to rest at the joining of her legs.

Even through the material, he could feel her heat. "Is that for me too?" he asked, gently mocking as he raised his head to look deep into her green eyes. He could see gold flecks there. His hand moved slowly, exploringly, and he felt his manhood stir in answer as she swallowed convulsively.

She wasted no more time. Her hands went right to his hips, only to be frustrated.

"O'Brien," she snarled, "get that damned cummerbund off before I tear it off with my teeth!"

He was, of course, laughing at her as he leaned back to remove the rest of his clothes, but she was past caring. At this point, Taylor was more than willing to trade some small part of her dignity for the feel of his skin on her own. Skin? His chest was nothing but dark soft fur, and her fingers itched to explore it . . . again.

Finally he stood before her in the semilight, her beautiful, beautiful man. She was awed by him. His power, his essence poured through every line of his body. She had teased him about his daily workouts, but they had made him hard and strong-muscled, as her own running kept her slender, her muscles taut.

Yes, she loved this man, but what she was feeling right now was that love combined with sheer lust for this magnificent male animal.

At the look in her eyes, he fell back to his knees and began to work impatiently at her trouser fastenings. She lifted slightly to aid him.

"You're not wearing anything underneath?" He stared at her incredulously.

"What for?" she responded with a twinkle.

He cleared his throat grumpily. "I'm sure glad I didn't know that all evening!" And he shook his head in disgust at how entertaining she found him. And she *was* entertained by these new facets of O'Brien's personality. That is, until he started running his hands downward along her thighs, pushing away the soft material as he went.

When he reached her ankles, he encircled them with his fingers before he swept the cloth from her. She still felt the impression of those fingers, almost to the bone, as he bent to bestow hot, wet kisses on one kneecap, then the other. Taylor shivered in reaction, and gasped at the unexpected pleasure. Her knees raised and parted slightly in reflex. She didn't have time to be self-conscious at her body's betrayal, because he was turning her slowly onto her stomach, leaving a moist trail of devastating kisses over the backs of her knees. He was moving them slowly up her thighs, sculpting each one with exquisite detail.

When he reached the curve of her buttocks, Taylor could stand no more. But as she tried to turn, O'Brien's hands went to her shoulders to hold her in place against the pillows. Her hands twisted in the bedclothes as she let him have his way, but she couldn't help the half-sob that escaped her in frustration.

He was nibbling the tender cheeks in slow-moving circles. And, when he was sure she would stay put, he began a secondary attack with his hands, caressing, kneading. Instinct guided him as he slid one hand down between her parted legs to find her hot and wet for him. The small cry she gave at his touch aroused him even further.

Deftly he slid his other hand under her stom-

ach and lifted her slightly to give his left hand more
room to tease. As she moved against him in
response, his nips and kisses became less controlled. Then her whole body suddenly stiffened in
pleasure. In control once more, he
slowed his movements until he was sure she was
back with him again.

Gently he turned her to him, only to find tears
in her eyes. Close in his arms, she whispered, "I
wanted it to be with you." She sounded so sad.

His chuckle was a low rumble. "We have all
night, love, I just wanted a proper introduction.
And"—he pulled back a ways to look into her eyes—
"believe me, that time *was* with me."

She buried her face in his damp neck and
tasted salt with her embarrassment. But he
wouldn't leave her be. He bent and kissed her hot
cheeks, then her lips. Then he moved down her
throat to find her pulse.

Mouth moving on her throat, he said in wonder, "How you can still blush after all this time . . ."
making her redden even more.

Taylor, feeling this attack was a bit one-sided,
suddenly reached over the side of the bed and
found her target with perfect aim. His gasp of surprise was quite satisfactory.

Once there, Taylor found his velvety softness
much too enticing too leave. And the raggedness of
O'Brien's breathing did nothing to discourage her.
She tugged him up and onto the bed with her with
one hand, still exploring with the other. His soft
skin sheathed an iron that was more than completely fascinating. Well, nothing changed here.
Heat flooded her as he moved in her hands, then
against her lips.

"Ah, love, I've wanted you, missed you," he

breathed as he pulled her back up to lie beside him. He was too far gone for that kind of play. He tried to think of times tables and icy water, but could only think of the warm, giving woman under him.

He buried his face in her neck and gave himself up to her scent. He wanted to taste her.

"You smell of the sea," she told him between kisses, but he only groaned and kissed her more deeply.

When she said, "I want to feel you inside me," he shuddered but shook his head slightly. "Not yet."

Despite her wordless protest, he ran little kisses down her body, stopping to tease her taut nipples. His warm mouth pulled at her, moving from one breast to the other until she squirmed under him. Then he moved downward, over her stomach, to where he knew she would be swollen for him. Just above that place he stopped. Then he moved to kneel between her parted legs.

"Yes, love," she said in a long sigh that made him smile. But he had more in mind than she.

Pulling one leg, then the other, over his shoulders, he bent to her, blocking out the light. At the first contact of his hot mouth upon her, however, she arched up in surprise. She wanted him *with* her, not just giving *her* pleasure.

He steadied her with both hands and said, "Shh, love, this way, this way. For me." And she gave in. He watched her head go back in anticipation as he bent once more to caress and tease her with lips and tongue.

It made her want to cry, to laugh, to scream, all at once. She wasn't even aware of her own body, only the rush of passion, of need he was creating.

The sounds she made sent a deep-felt satisfaction running through him. He loved giving her this. But now, just now, he wanted to watch her face.

He shifted, placing a pillow beneath her hips. Loving this, measuring her experience by each change of expression, he led her onward. Then, as her hips arched even higher, he suddenly pulled away, only to bury his manhood deep within her.

"O'Brien!" she cried out, reminding him of the first time. He didn't move for a long moment, savoring the intensity, until he had almost pushed himself too far. When he did move, it was with long, slow strokes that warmed them both. Then, too soon, he was gone, only to return with his mouth upon her again. He was sending her right to the edge, but she wanted it never to end.

He could feel her readiness. Taylor was twisting against him in need, and he knew he couldn't last much longer.

He came into her once more, stoking the fire with more energy, more hunger. Just before he lost control, he left her again. Their breathing loud in his ears, he heard Taylor give a little sob. Her hands were curled tightly in the sheets, her head moving from side to side. "O'Brien, come to me, please, come to me. I can't stand any more."

"Soon, love, soon," he answered, breathing hard. "First you come to me." And she laughed weakly, ending with a low moan as he continued his caresses.

So gently, so expertly he took her. Whispering his name for her, he took her up with him. Caught on the verge of that ecstasy, Taylor reached blindly for his shoulders to pull him to her. "Please, please . . ." She *needed* him inside her. His whole body trembling with his own need, O'Brien came into her again with one deep thrust. His body arched . . . such heat!

Then she cried out in a high voice, and Sean felt her stiffen. "Oh, Sean . . . oh, love . . ." His arms tightened about her convulsively as he withdrew, then plunged again, savoring her muscles still contracting strongly around him.

How good they were together, he thought, and how he loved her. Then he could take no more; she was driving him out of his mind. Burying himself deep within her, he rolled over until she was upon him. Her wild red hair was everywhere, her lips and cheeks on fire. At last, with no words, no sense, he, too, cried out, lifting her high with the arch of his body before he rolled her under him once more, clutching her tightly to him.

"Woman, sweet woman, what you do to me!" he muttered hoarsely when he could speak. "Nothing and no one else comes close."

"For me too," she answered sweetly, rubbing her face on his furry chest. But soon he felt the wetness of her tears, and bent to her in concern, cupping her chin in his big hand.

"Did I hurt you, love?" he queried gently. "Was I too rough?"

Her watery chuckle answered him. "No more than I, my bear. But . . . I've missed you," she finished simply. And she couldn't have said another word, for he was squeezing the very breath from her. Moments passed, full and quiet, before she felt his lips on hers once more. Something lovely flowed between them.

Trying to lighten the mood before she said

something stupid, Taylor pulled herself from his arms and glanced downward.

"Something on your mind, Sleeping Beauty?" she teased.

"Oh, no, you don't," O'Brien cautioned, pulling her back to him with a squeeze from behind, exciting her all over again with that single move. "One kiss woke me. Now it's your responsibility to finish the job!"

"Oh, well," she returned petulantly, "aaaallll right, but this wasn't in the book *I* got."

"Fine print," he retaliated without a qualm.

And that was the last thing either of them said for a long, long time.

Seven

Morning came, and with it came a host of unwelcome thoughts.

Taylor had wakened at first light, held loosely in O'Brien's arms. She took a moment to enjoy the sight of his unshaven, sleep-softened face.

Taking care not to rouse him, she slipped gingerly from the bed and made her way to the bathroom. Once there, she decided that she would bathe downstairs and let O'Brien sleep a bit longer. Besides, she needed time away from the sight of that little-boy face to be able to straighten out her thoughts. So she collected what she would need and tiptoed down, grabbing cut-offs and a Yankees T-shirt on the way.

Strange, her body felt strong and frail at the same time. Unused muscles pulled at her as she moved, and there was a certain soreness in her nether regions. But, overall, her body was filled with a terrific sense of well-being. Not so her mind.

"What have I done?" she berated herself in a small voice. She knew that O'Brien was bound to wake with the idea that life would go back to predivorce routine, but she couldn't allow that to happen.

Of course, she had no intention of letting O'Brien get away. She loved him to distraction— appropriate term, that. However, there was quite a lot to be gone over between them before what occurred last night could be allowed to happen again.

No, much as she would love to have him in her bed every night, and hard as he would be to resist, *first* would have to come a much clearer understanding between them.

Ahh, but it had been . . .

"Get hold of yourself, girl," she admonished herself lightly. "How are you going to explain this to O'Brien if you weaken in your own thoughts?" On the other hand, she didn't know whether he might not be planning to have the same talk with her.

As much as she would have liked a morning run, she felt she needed the time to think. And she didn't want O'Brien waking to find her gone, not after last night.

Remembering in flashes, she couldn't help the blush that suffused her face, even alone. No, she wasn't ready to face O'Brien's scrutiny, just yet, anyway.

So she showered, changed, and, morning-fresh, went to make coffee. In the living room, she let Vivaldi violins wash over her as she tried to organize a plan of action.

She was sipping coffee on the couch, eyes on the tree branches visible through the open window, when she heard O'Brien's soft tread on the stairs behind her.

"Coffee!" he groaned in mock agony, leaning over the back of the couch, hands on her shoulders.

"Good morning," she said, chin held high, her voice suddenly husky.

His hands tightened upon her as she looked up at him over her right shoulder. "Just what I need to revive me," he said thankfully before he leaned down to bestow a morning-tender kiss upon her.

Aah, bliss, she thought. Was it possible to fight a man who had such intuitive knowledge of what a woman needed? Well, maybe it was beyond her weight, but she had to *try*, at least.

Opening her mouth, however, she was expertly cut off. *This* kiss was only used to shut her mouth before he begged, "Honey, I know we have to talk, but please . . . coffee first?" Unhappy at being manipulated, but knowing that his request was only fair, Taylor managed a regal nod. "Please-sir-I-want-summore?" She posed, waving her cup, before he grabbed it with a mock-stern face and made for the scullery.

His return brought on all the chumminess that drinking morning coffee to sunlight and Vivaldi could manufacture. What was that phrase, now . . . the luck of the Irish?

"Well," he said finally from the easy chair across from her.

"Well," she echoed.

"Uh . . . yeah . . ." he said, pushing his tongue into his cheek. "Well!" he said again, this time with enthusiasm.

"I believe we already covered that subject," replied Our Miss Brooks before she laid down the law. "I'm warning you right now, O'Brien—don't make me laugh! You do, and it's curtains!"

He was choking pathetically on his coffee, but he knew better than to let her know it, so he swallowed nobly, and with difficulty. Taylor had the damnedest way of reusing clichés and jigsawing metaphors.

"I guess we'd better get down to it." Now Taylor was back, even if she did carry a trace of Bella Abzug.

"I know you've worked up a plan," he said for openers, "something sort of celibate, I presume?"

"Sort of. You game?" His answer would show what kind of chance they might have, and she waited for it, unable to disguise her feelings completely.

"Well," he countered, "I think I'd like to hear you out before I incriminate myself."

"Um-hmm," was her only answer for a moment, before she took her life in her hands. "Yeah, I'll see what I can do to make you an offer you can't refuse." Then she narrowed her eyes and sent a stern look right to his baby blues. "O'Brien, you dog, don't make me premise this conversation with how much last night meant to me, or how special it was." There she stopped and scrutinized him. "Or am I alone here?"

Well, at least he had the grace to look a little shamed, along with pleased. "Red, it was special and important to me, and the very best thing that's happened to me since I . . . since we . . . uh, yeah." O'Brien dug a great hole. "But"—he was suddenly back on top—"the only way I know to *really* reassure you would be to repeat the experience, which I would be *happy* to do, but"—he was watching her expression—"I somehow feel that is not on your immediate agenda."

"Treading on thin ice, O'Brien."

"I'll be good, truly. Only, put that look away. It throws my timing off."

He just couldn't stop the roll he was on—the brat. But she knew how to handle him. Not a word, not a move; she let one raised eyebrow say it all.

"Oops." His head ducked down in penitence. "Well, at least I'll *try*. . . ."

Damn him! He *knew* she couldn't resist a hurt pup! "Have some coffee, you big baby," she suggested, relenting, "then we'll try to talk again."

So they had coffee.

Taylor found herself staring out the front window, full of love for him and trying to formulate an explanation of her ideas. But her mind kept going blank. After a few more minutes she turned to O'Brien and realized he had been watching her. She jumped right in.

"Um—yes . . . well, is there anything you want to say before we get into it?"

He simply shook his head, putting her back on the spot.

"Okay, then, here goes. Just a stab in the dark, and I wasn't going to ask this, but I think we have to talk about why you really left."

He blinked owlishly. This was not what he had expected to hear. But she did have a right to an explanation. He studied her for a moment, her face carefully devoid of expression. Now, for Taylor, whose face was a picture that matched every thought, that very stillness carried its own message, and well he knew it.

He took a deep breath, wiped his hands on the

worn knees of his jeans, and set his jaw at a peculiar angle. "I came back, you know," he said—flooring her—"but you had already gone." He tried, but couldn't completely camouflage, the accusation in his eyes.

"When?" she asked in a gritty voice, unable to say more.

"I don't know exactly. I drove north for hours. I found myself near the woods when I needed gas. I walked. The trees were beautiful, so green and peaceful. When I finally cooled down, I realized how silly it had all been. Then I drove back." O'Brien took another long breath and let it out slowly. His eyes revealed the hurt inside him. "I thought we'd just had a fight . . . Red, how did it all get so important?"

"I don't know, love. I don't know. I was quite sure you'd only taken a walk. Then, after hours and hours of waiting, when it turned daylight and you still hadn't come home . . . all I could remember was the look in your eyes and the sound of your voice saying how tired you were. Oh, dammit, all the things you said kept running through my mind like a litany of my flaws. I was sure you'd, well, that you'd had enough." Tears were in her voice now, and edging to the corners of her eyes. He started toward her, but her tightened lips stopped him. She fought for control enough to steady her breathing. Somehow it seemed very important to get all of it out. "You'd never left me before, O'Brien. When we fought, we'd yell, then we'd sometimes laugh." She had no dignity, no sense of pride, she hated herself, but she had to ask. "Why did you stop loving me?"

He was stunned. She'd done it again, taken him totally and completely by surprise. That was the last thing he would have imagined was in her mind when he left.

"My God, Taylor, I didn't! I never stopped loving you! I was an ass. I was confused. Our life was becoming such a race, I blamed everyone for everything. But I never once thought you'd believe I had gone for good. Hell, I didn't even take a suitcase!"

"You started to," she accused, glaring at him through eyes that refused to either overflow or stop tearing.

"Just temper—it was that or break things." He raked a hand through his thick hair. "It wasn't even all us, Red. I had backed myself into a corner financially by investing in the play I was directing. Then, I would never give myself a day off. The strongest characters in the play were miscast, and everything—from set design to costumes to publicity—everything was behind schedule and over budget. I never got to see you, and when I did, you were either distracted, working in the study, or already asleep. It was hell on my peace of mind as well as my anatomy. So when we started fighting . . . I was just so mad at all of it . . ." He leaned forward in his chair, across the space that separated them, to run a finger down her chin.

"I felt the same way," she said softly as her head bent. "I knew you weren't interested in Trace. But once it started I couldn't help myself. I was an earthquake waiting to happen." Soberly she continued. "I think I would have done almost anything to make you notice me again."

Then he was beside her, squeezing her to him, his arms tightening with every word. "I think we've both been idiots who don't deserve the second chance we've been given." He pulled away and looked deep into her eyes with those blue lights of

105

his own. "I guess I don't have to tell you that I love you very much."

Tell me, *tell* me! That look warmed her to her toes.

"I've missed you like hell, every damned minute!" Then he sighed in one sharp burst before he turned his face to the window. "You know, I used to see a woman on the street who would walk like you and I would be a monster for days on the set."

"You won't believe it." Taylor gave a wry grin, catching his attention. "The same thing would happen to me. But I was luckier. Not many men could match that bean-pole stride!"

"If you're going to start calling me names, we'll have to strip and compare muscles," he went on as she sputtered into one warm shoulder. "But just now, honey, I want to get past this big plan of yours."

"Okay, but you sit on your side of the couch, and let me get through as much as I can." She looked him in the eye. "Yes?"

"Yes, all right. If my presence *so* destroys your, shall we call it, ability, to think?" He moved.

Mmm, so smug. Taylor set her face seriously and began. "It's really no big plan, more the order of things, or the pace I think we should take. I think it should be slower." Don't look at him, don't dare, she cautioned herself. "No matter what we've had, what we've been to each other, a year has passed, and our lives have changed. You've become a film director, and I . . ." Her voice dropped off as she tried to think of a way to describe the changes that had taken place in her career, in her life.

But before she could speak again, he interrupted softly. "And you've gotten a lot of recognition. I know how that can change a life, Red. And I also know you're trying to point out obstacles between us. Obstacles that don't really exist, if we want to work around them."

She looked at him, leaning forward in his chair, eyes watching her carefully. Was he waiting for her to commit herself? She hoped not. And there was something that she still had to say. She took a deep breath.

"You left me, O'Brien. Just walked out. And, as much as I would like to believe you intended to come back, I'm not sure that I do." His answer was immediate, and stinging.

"You *divorced* me, Taylor. You picked up your marbles and went home. At this point I don't quite trust you either." She knew she deserved that. But when she looked up at him again, the anger she had seen in his eyes was replaced by something else she didn't dare put a label on. "I think," he went on, his wonderful eyes never leaving hers, "that we were both very proud and very childish. I want another crack at it."

She was silent for what seemed to him to be a long time, before she finally exhaled with a long breath and warned, "We'll fight. There's a lot we disagree about in any production, and especially this one."

He was careful not to smile, though he felt like it. This moment was too important. "There's always brute force." He shrugged lightly, dismissingly.

She looked down quickly and went on. "And, umm, about . . . well, I can't very well tell you not to touch me. That would be ridiculous. But I think we ought to go back to square two or three and start over. This has just all happened so fast, Sean." She looked at the grain of the fabric of the couch, measured its pillows, saw that the ficus tree needed watering. She relearned that room in twenty seconds, before she finally gave O'Brien a quick glance. "So whaddya think?" Why was he taking so long? When he did finally speak, she couldn't have been more surprised.

"Okay," he said simply.

She did a double take. He couldn't have faked how much he wanted her last night. Not so many times. He'd been as hungry for her as he had been during the first week of their relationship, when he would grab her at odd times in odd places, with that look in his eye. Why was he giving in so easily? It wasn't at all like O'Brien.

He looked wistfully toward the curving area of her T-shirt.

Damn it, if she would remember to wear a bra, this wouldn't always be happening to her—or at least he wouldn't see it! But, bless the man, he never once referred to the very obvious fact that they had met each other upon equal ground.

"I don't *like* it." Well, that mollified her somewhat. "I've just got the taste of you back in my senses." *That* sent her over the edge—too many images. "But"—he went on as if he hadn't seen her gulping air—"if you'll concede a little lighthearted necking"—she'd have to be a three-year-old to believe in *that* with O'Brien—"now and then to . . . uh . . . fix my perspective, I *might* just be able to handle it . . . for a while. I want you back, Red," he said with an intensity that did her heart good. "We'll eventually work it out your way. But you're gonna miss me up there." He pointed at the ceiling and gave her a look that pushed her heart rate to a dangerous level. "Anyway," he continued, "if your way doesn't work, I'll just tie you to the bed till you cry, 'Uncle.' "

At that Taylor stuck two fingers in her luke-warm coffee and flicked them at his face. "Down, Rover, down."

That day Taylor decided it was time to tackle the two people she had been fending off since Sean's appearance.

First she had to call her mother. If any more time passed before *she* found out, or if, God forbid, O'Brien should answer the phone when she called . . . well, it would make a difficult situation worse.

Naturally, her mother was home. She was *never* home during the day. *And* she had plenty of time to talk.

When Taylor began, and she began haltingly, the silence on the other end of the wire was not overly encouraging. But when she was done with her scrappy story, her mother didn't even put up a fight.

"You're sure you know what you're doing, dear?" was all that she said in answer.

"Uhm, well . . . no . . ." she responded, "I'm hoping things will just work themselves out." Then she went on stumblingly, "He seems to really want to try, Mom . . . and I want to too."

"Then, do it. I trust your judgment, Taylor. Just know that I'm here if you need to talk, or anything."

"Thanks, Mom . . . for making it so easy on me."

She didn't pretend to misunderstand, but just said, "I love you, dear. Call me in a week or so and let me know how things are going."

"Okay. I love you too. 'Bye."

" 'Bye."

When the phone clicked, Taylor stared at it for almost a full minute before replacing it carefully in the cradle. She felt like a guilty prisoner given an undeserved reprieve. She had been so prepared for warnings and arguments that her mother's gentle understanding threw her completely.

"Well, I'll be damned," she muttered to herself. Then, hoping to ride on the streak of luck she had obviously been granted, Taylor picked up the phone again and dialed. Her eyes shut and fingers crossed, she heard the phone being picked up just before she heard the sound of that dreaded voice. "Hello?"

"Uhm, Rhea?" she managed to squeak out.

"Hi, Tay, i was wondering when you were going to get around to me. Lunch?"

"Mmm hmm." Buck up, girl, it wasn't the dentist, after all! "Le Parc okay?"

"Fine. One o'clock all right with you?"

"Sure. See you then." Then she hung up with lightning speed before she could chicken out.

Rhea had known her much too long and was not going to be satisfied with simple explanations. She would want to know everything.

Eight

Le Parc was a chic, quiet little place over-looking Central Park's west side. The *maître d'* was quite used to such spectacles as Taylor presented when she exited from the elevator, but he still enjoyed some of them; this was one.

Dressed in a sleek, pearl-gray ultrasuede suit with pale gray suede boots, her bright hair drew more than a few glances. She was working very hard to present the picture of innocence wronged.

As she was led to a window table, she avoided Rhea's knowing eye until she was actually seated. Then, when she saw that Rhea was wearing bright and flowing peacock blue in contrast, she had to laugh.

"The battle begins! A costumer couldn't have done better." She grinned into Rhea's big, sparkling eyes.

"That's true," Rhea answered with her own

wide, rueful smile. "But I hope I'm not truly cast as the guillotine to your innocent aristo." She waited a moment before she went on. "Really, Tay, you don't have to tell me anything if you don't want to. I *am* on your side, you know."

"I know, Ree, I know. It's just that once I've told you . . . well . . . I guess I feel that that will be the signal that I'm really committed to this." Then she gave a twisted grin and paraphrased, "This 'whatever it is.'"

"Well, let's order a bottle of wine, and you can drive me crazy with the suspense until you're tiddly enough that it all pours out without your noticing."

"*D'accord, chérie,*" Taylor responded, squirming in the soft chair to settle herself for the next hour or two. "You are truly an understanding friend."

After two glasses of champagne—they had decided that eating would really be a waste of precious time—Rhea pounced.

"So . . . was it as good as ever?"

"Now, *there's* a subtle opening," Taylor chastised.

"It *was*," Rhea accused single-mindedly.

"Mmm hmmm." Taylor allowed herself a tiny smile of memory, then felt obliged to set the record straight. "It was better."

"Really?" Rhea was amused.

"Shut up, you. What kind of friend are you, anyway, making fun of my tender romance?" Then she plunged onward. "I made him make a deal with me to go more . . . um . . . slowly for a while. I'm wondering how I'll survive it."

Rhea *was* a good friend, but at this she couldn't stop the laughter that poured out. Shaking her head, she teased, "I only wish I could have been a fly on the wall to see just who was seducing 'who-um'!"

Taylor pursed her lips in answer and stared vaguely out the window, ignoring the view below. She let her green eyes meet Rhea's big brown ones. "It was a toss-up."

"So what happens now?" Rhea was pouring more champagne.

"You know as much as I do. You tell me." Taylor was feeling mighty comfy at this point as she slipped a leg under herself and resettled.

"Well, said the doctor, what do you *want* to happen?"

"Rhea, you idiot, I want him back!" Taylor placed her chin in hand to continue. "I just want to be sure."

"Of what, exactly?"

"That we can make it, that he really wants me, that he won't leave at the first sign of trouble, that he's the same man I fell in love with, *all* of the above."

"Hmmm. Well, how long are you going to hold him off?"

She really *did* have a one-track mind. Taylor gave a little giggle. "I don't know. I guess it depends on how long we can both stand it, or how close we get." She looked up with a mischievous gleam in her eyes. "However, he *did* say something about tying me to the bed if it takes too long."

A few heads did turn at the waterfalls of laughter coming from the corner table where the two sophisticated-looking, champagne-filled beauties were sitting, but *they* didn't notice a thing.

Rhea leaned over the table, one hand supporting her, and hissed in speculation, "What do you think—handcuffs or silk scarves?"

"Actually"—Taylor recrossed her legs in concentration—"I think a stoppable pulley would be the most practical idea, but silk is really the most romantic."

Rhea lifted her glass in the air. "To the romantic Irish," she toasted before she gave a devil's grin, "and to silk."

"I hate you, Rhea," Taylor muttered, but she drank. "Now"—she placed her empty glass carefully on the tablecloth and gave a wide smile of anticipation—"let's talk about *your* love life."

During the next few weeks, Sean and Taylor put "The Plan" into action and to the test. The first two weeks were the hardest, when the memory of what they were denying themselves was the strongest. But they were full of resolution to make things work between them.

Rehearsals had begun, and were going smooth as glass. Whenever they got to the end of the third act, they rehearsed both endings. O'Brien had hounded her for a week to write the other ending so they could try both.

Taylor was wonderfully patient with her costar, and even the extra rehearsals with just the two of them were going well.

Never were such sweet words spoken.

Of course, neither Sean nor Taylor noticed the crew's wariness of this newfound calm. *They* were accustomed to heated discussion and small battles. Now, along with Rhea and O'Malley, they were waiting for the other shoe to fall.

After eight, when rehearsals were over for the day, they went home to the cozy brownstone.

Taylor had started cooking O'Brien's dinner every night. Who would have believed it? Certainly no one was more surprised than he. And—the saints be praised!—Taylor showed a fine talent for following written orders. *And* she had cunning enough to have a frozen meal waiting in case of disaster. Well, it had only happened twice.

After the first night, Sean would go to the corner for flowers and then stand, looking like an overgrown sixteen-year-old, holding them until she took them from him with a shy kiss.

This little ritual so pleased them both that after a week it was still in effect.

Finally, one night, after Taylor had looked in vain for *another* vase, she ended up back in the flower-bedecked living room.

Facing a surprised O'Brien, she threw her arms wide with helplessness and suppressed merriment. Finally she overflowed, tossing the daisies high.

"Oh, Sean, look at us," she gurgled, "*I* hate to cook and *you*'ve sunk as low as daisies." Her hand went to her mouth in an effort at self-control. "You're *allergic* to daisies!"

He was beautiful when he blushed, just beautiful.

"Pax?" she asked gently, when she could.

"Thank heaven for a practical woman!" His embarrassment was sweet to her eyes. "What do you say we hop a cab to Chinatown?"

"I would be just too, too delighted!" Then she looked down at herself. "Only, let me rid myself of this appendage." She referred to her voluminous butcher's apron. It was the only kind large enough to protect her from her mistakes. She couldn't resist fluttering her eyelashes over her shoulder as she made for the kitchen, leaving O'Brien to gather up the daisies with an odd sneeze or two.

She waited until he put them down and picked up his glass before she delivered her parting shot.

"I was on my way out of recipes and moving fast toward Rhea's halibut mousse, so we both lucked out."

O'Brien really did choke beautifully, even if it *was* a waste of good wine.

Taylor had always thought that there was something very special and otherworldly, almost storybooklike, about Chinatown. No matter how many tourists poured over its streets, they and their languages remained only background. Chinatown reeked of the Orient, decadence, and poverty, beauty and garbage, children playing on the streets long after dark, and silent, middle-aged women making their way through the crowds. The perfect setting for a spy novel—if somewhat cli- chéd. It was marvelous!

By the time their cab had made the short leap into this other world, the streets had become slick and shiny-black with summer rain, the lights made even brighter by contrast.

Her arm held tightly in O'Brien's, they made their way through the maze of people to their favor- ite restaurant, eyes wide in appreciation of all the sights.

Suddenly Taylor pulled on O'Brien's arm with a sharp jerk, dragging him into the open doorway of one of the multitude of tiny shops filled with tourist glitter. Some of it was even from China.

The "candy-store syndrome" was strong in Taylor, and well Sean knew it. But he tagged along patiently as she pored over shelves with gluttonous delight. She rarely bought anything in these stores or in the junk shops where she foraged uptown. But she loved to look, and on a rare occasion . . .

O'Brien was around a corner buying her a pair of patterned ballet slippers when she saw them.

In a small, dusty glass case held closed by a clumsy padlock were five small jade figures. "Nichi" was the name of these little characters, a friend had once told her. Quietly, with a glance to see where O'Brien was wandering, she bought the one that laughed; a fat, squatting figure carved in exquisite detail.

She paid far more than she would have expected, but she was unwilling to bargain with the tiny, frail old man who wrapped and tied the figure with such care.

O'Brien and she met at the front door, both bursting with nonchalance—and triumph—and both mysteriously clutching a parcel.

Their eyes met in special understanding. This was an occasion.

Over fiery Szechuan food in their favorite restaurant they made a pact to keep each other from going overboard. No, they would never go too far, ever again.

"Sure . . ." they whined in unison.

That was the night they both stretched their willpower. They were in such lovely accord, not speaking whole sentences of conversation amid others. But for the buzz of conversation around them, and for all they knew, they might have been completely alone. They both felt the new magic, atop the old.

"We got any popcorn? *The Quiet Man* is on TV tonight," O'Brien said over fortune cookies.

Ah, the man knew the very best bait, she thought.

Her eyes had glazed with their "old movie" light, and O'Brien ushered her out while she was still in a silent daze of anticipation.

She suddenly came alive. "But my fortune!"

"I've got it," O'Brien returned, "and when I'm ready I might even let *you* read it."

"You, you treacherous, sneaking, thieving, traitorous rat fink," she grated out at him.

"Here!" he answered, hand raised innocently, and a yellow cab miraculously pulled to a stop at the curb.

"How'd you do that?" Taylor demanded suspiciously. "You know they almost never come right into Chinatown."

"Natural ability," he responded smugly.

"Swift kick at three o'clock, E.T.A. thirty seconds," Taylor announced cheekily, eyebrows to heaven, then with eyes on her nonexistent watch.

"Take cover!" he finished as he pushed her through the car door to the far side of the cab. "Ah-hah!" he announced from somewhere directly over her, "the enemy is immobilized!"

"No, suffocated!" she answered, her voice muffled by layers of O'Brien.

"Where to, Mac?" the cabbie demanded.

Taylor saw a reprieve as Sean gave their address to the driver.

Painfully extricating herself from underneath miles of Irishman, she harrumphed loudly.

"If you only knew the weight of what you throw

around so easily . . . O'Brien! I don't want to hear it, I don't even want to see it!"

So he schooled his expression. Such a shame, though, he thought, it *was* such a *perfect* lead in . . .

Nine

They ended up on the couch—of course, it didn't *start* that way—wallowing in popcorn and great character study.

First thing, when they came through the door, Taylor ran to the clock in the downstairs bedroom to see how much of the movie they might have missed.

Sean strolled to the kitchen with their left-overs. He knew the movie hadn't started yet. He put on the popcorn, then met Taylor in the living room, where she was plumping pillows and organizing the position of the television with savage intensity. Stage set, she gave it one last check, and then turned without a word and ran upstairs to change clothes. By the time she returned, the popcorn was ready and it was two minutes to countdown. She had her entrance timed to the second. O'Brien had planted himself on one corner of the long couch, hoping to avoid the whirlwind until it settled, which it did, right on his lap.

"This," stated the lady in the peach silk caftan, "is a lovely way to spend an evening!" His arms snaked around her to finish properly the kiss of gratitude she had started.

"Mmmm," said her romantic prince, "we got any beer in the fridge?"

"Back to the pond, you toad!" she ordered. "I'm expecting a frog with potential any minute!"

"Potential, huh?" This was the opening he had been waiting for.

But she was wise to him and clamped a hand over his mouth before he could make contact. "If I miss even the credits, you'll be cleaning the bathrooms for Angela for a month!"

"I give up! I give up!"

"Good! Then, turn it on and get the beer! Ooops!" She had just been speedily dumped on the carpet—but he *did* go get the beer.

When he came back from the kitchen, she was sitting cross-legged, staring with complete concentration at the credits of a film she had seen twenty times, as mesmerized now as any time before.

He stood in the doorway, a beer can in each hand, and muttered under his breath, "That's my girl!" Then he came forward to insinuate himself next to her.

At her first belly laugh he finally got her attention. She had to see his reaction, share hers with him.

He didn't disappoint her, and by the time Maureen O'Hara was dipping her hand in John Wayne's at the chapel, Taylor and Sean were sitting in each other's arms, chuckling with delight.

Sharing pleasure is a very dangerous aphrodisiac. By the time John was dragging Maureen through the hills, Taylor was fighting off some very strong impulses. And O'Brien was making no secret of his own.

"What are you doing?" Taylor demanded over her shoulder with what he judged to be only mild indignation.

"Uhmm, this is called nuzzling, if you want to be technical," he breathed over one ear, "and this is nipping," he went on as he traced the shape of her ear with his teeth. "And"—he finished as she gasped—"I think we could call this groping." She assumed he referred to the stray hand she found lightly fondling her breast.

Slowly, teasingly, he pinched the nipple through the soft silk. She forced herself to still the urge to arch against that hand.

"Yes," she answered with some difficulty. "I would definitely call that groping . . . or . . . third-year biology." With her last words, she felt a sudden surge against one buttock and cocked an eyebrow over her shoulder in his direction.

"Did I say anything?" he asked, slightly annoyed.

"Did you have to?"

"Very funny," he retaliated. "But you've had some 'speaking' moments yourself, if I recall." Then he pulled her right up against him, both of them still facing the movie, and wrapped his arms around her so that both hands could destroy her concentration. And, with one of his lightning changes of mood, he nodded toward the screen.

"Each character is given his or her moment to express his essence with poignance or humor. It's fantastic."

"It creates a life totally apart from the script or

events," she agreed. Then she turned in his arms. "O'Brien, do you think we could work with that premise on *The Run*?" Her excitement was obvious.

"We're talking about camera work, Red," he said with a frown.

"Yes and no. I think we're talking about focus." She moved to sit beside him. Suddenly she dropped her bombshell. "I want a week, O'Brien."

Uh-oh, he thought, there was that light in her eyes. "What?" he didn't move.

"I want to take a week away from rehearsals and rewrite from this angle." She didn't move either. She waited for the explosion.

"You want me to suspend the *entire* production so that you can rewrite this *entire* play?" He was incredulous. "No," he said after a moment, "absolutely not." He turned and took her shoulders in his hands. "Red, think about it! We are talking about the cost of the three weeks we've already put into the production, the week *you* want for rewrites and whatever adjustment time it would take afterward."

"O'Brien." Her tone was low, dangerous. "I don't think I need a lecture on production costs at this point."

"Red, who do you expect to deal with the backers?"

Yes, oh, yes, he was right. O'Brien would be the one who would have to explain to the big boys.

"Okay," she said, "I'll be sick for a week."

"What?" he roared.

"Your choice," she said quietly.

"I don't believe you're doing this." He ran his hand roughly through his hair. "This is unheard of, it's unprofessional!"

That was the ultimate insult! They were no longer in each other's arms, but facing each other. Adversaries.

"Don't start, O'Brien. Just listen to me a minute first." She took a deep breath, saw that he was waiting, not with an exactly receptive look on his face, but he *was* giving her the time to explain her idea. "All you'd have to stop would be rehearsals; production plans wouldn't be affected at all. I know this is sudden." She ignored that snort he gave. "But I know it will work, and the depth it will add to the play will be worth it."

She stared into his eyes then, willing his understanding. "O'Brien, I *know* this will work. I know it will be good. Please. I need this week. If it takes longer, I'll can the idea or work the rest out in advance of the rehearsal."

He stared at her long and hard. It was impulsive, harebrained, but he knew she was serious. He was also quite sure that she would manage to get her week whether he agreed or not. Some director! Damn, she made him mad! He started slowly, carefully. "Do you really think it's wise to make this major a decision in the space of, what, five minutes?" She started to open her mouth, but he went on. "Some people would call this 'self-destruction,' while others might call it 'temperament.' "

"What would you call it?" she asked quietly, steeling herself for his answer.

"I'm not quite sure." His face was carefully controlled. "Ask me again when your week is up."

"O'Brien!" She wanted to throw her arms around him, but his expression stopped her. "You'll agree!"

"Would it make a difference one way or the

other?" Her face fell in shame. He was right—she would do it anyway. "I don't appreciate the position you're putting me in professionally, Taylor. And"—he went on in a hard voice—"I don't appreciate the blackmail."

Lord, he was right, she thought. She was terrible.

"But," he went on, "since you are bound and determined, I'll just say this. Don't ever pull a stunt like this again."

Her stomach dropped with a heavy feeling of dread. O'Brien's respect was something she prized highly, and she knew she had lost a bit of it with her hijinks. But, dammit, this play was her baby, and it deserved the absolute best she could give it. That much she owed to herself and to the play. So the timing was lousy. That was just too bad. She had no choice.

As she felt the thickness of the wall that had fallen between them, she wanted to cry, but she wouldn't. She wasn't wrong, she *wasn't*.

She looked down at her hands, clenched in her lap. She had pressed the thin silk of her caftan into accordion pleats. "I'll call Rhea and see if I can borrow her cabin upstate. It takes about two hours to get there."

"I know," he said with no expression; her face flooded with color as she remembered the weekend they had spent there one winter. Now, though, she was getting tired of being punished by this attitude of his. He didn't have to rub it in—she had gotten the message. He was mad, and he was hurt.

"There's no phone in the cabin," he reminded her. His voice was still hard, measured.

"I know. I won't need one." She could be just as

tough and offhand as he. "I'll just be writing. The fewer interruptions, the better."

"Yeah." His face looked like stone. What had she said now? Why couldn't he just hold her, kiss her, have faith in her?

"You'll need the car, or would you rather I drove you up?"

His voice had lightened a bit, and she was grateful for the offer. She had to stop this horrible tension in the air somehow. So she reached a hand across the ocean of space between them and rested it on top of his. His darkened eyes met hers. "Thank you. I didn't want to have to ask for the car." His hand turned over under hers. With his palm warm against hers, they finally made contact.

"C'mere," was all he said as he pulled her to him. And with her head buried against his great chest she was finally able to take a normal breath. His arms were tightening, crushing her, but she didn't care. When she lifted her head, his eyes met hers with a hunger she knew was echoed in her own. She didn't give a damn that he would see it there.

When he bent to kiss her, she arched up to meet him, opening her mouth to take his with an urgency that expressed her need. Her hands ran over his shoulders, kneading hard muscles that had grown tense in this last half hour. His hands were running up and down her back, sliding over her with ease, using the silk of her caftan like the softest gloves, to electrify her skin.

Their need to recapture their earlier closeness was sending them both out of control with lightning speed.

When his hands moved to shape her breasts,

Taylor's head went back with a low moan. He replaced one hand with his mouth, drawing on the nipple through the silk; his other hand went to the hem of the caftan and under, to run up her leg and squeeze her thigh.

Her hands were in his soft dark hair, then running over his shoulders and down his arms. She knew every line and sinew, but she needed to touch him, to feel every pore in his skin.

He was still teasing at one breast when she leaned to place a kiss on his neck. She couldn't resist a taste with her tongue or still the busy hands on the buttons of his shirt until, thinking of something even more interesting, she let one hand reach down to caress him through his jeans.

"Oh, Red." He groaned; eyes closed.

"Yes, love, yes," she answered as her hands went to the snap of his jeans. Their hands met in a tangle as each tried to rid the other of unnecessary clothing. For a moment they fell apart laughing at themselves and their obvious, if not graceful, urgency.

Then Taylor took O'Brien's face gently in her trembling hands and looked into his big, long-lashed blue eyes and said, "I need you, Sean." And she hoped he knew she meant for more than this moment or making love.

He answered first with eyes grown tender and then with his mouth, which settled gently on hers. He kissed her with small, fragile kisses over and over before he trailed those kisses to her ear and whispered fiercely, "And I need *you*, Red."

She couldn't help the small cry that escaped her as she leaped at him, pushing him down on the couch until she lay full length upon him. She wrapped both arms around his neck in a stranglehold and let her kisses say all she couldn't say with words. His hands had gotten under the caftan and grabbed her tightly to him as he arched upward. Then he was moving the silk up and over her head.

"I'm doing the best I can, O'Brien," she said finally. "But these tight jeans have gotten tighter, and they don't want to let you go."

He chuckled and then dumped her sideways on the couch as he rose to remove them. Eyeing her steadily, he did a slow striptease. Taylor lay on one elbow as she watched with mock calm. "You're not wearing anything underneath?" she asked, remembering.

"What for?" he answered with a lopsided grin. Slowly he turned away from the heat in her eyes to turn off the television and one of the lamps. Then he picked up the long coffee table and moved it against one wall. She was definitely intrigued.

Next he lay down on the carpet in front of the couch and placed his hands behind his head, looking ridiculous in his unconcern with one part of him standing at attention.

"Come to me," he murmured, his eyes on the ceiling.

"My prince." She sighed in resigned response as she made her way to him.

But all teasing ended when she knelt above him, sitting on her heels, and told him stories with her eyes. He didn't move, but held his breath as she let her hands run, unimpeded, down his chest, over his narrow hips, to meet where he pulsed in her hands. Filled with awe, her lips ran the same path, loving him, loving how he moved under her, as if he couldn't control his response to her touch. His ragged breathing filled the air of her world with sound, exciting her even more.

Suddenly he pulled away, then grabbed her with his hands at her waist, making her gasp as he simply lifted her in the air, positioned them both, and let her slide down over him.

Her breath escaped in a half-sob, half-sigh, but he held her hard against him, and still, by his hands on her hips.

His eyes squeezed tightly shut, he held his breath for a moment before whispering, "Not yet, don't move yet." He released a long breath and let his hands run up her sides to her breasts, then over her stomach, down through the crisp curls, to tease her with both thumbs. He felt her contract around him at his touch and smiled up at her. "You gonna miss me while you're gone?" But she only answered with a small sound as her head fell to one side and she began to move.

Ten

They made love twice again that night, the last time with slow and tender passion. After the third time they slept, still on the living-room floor.

O'Brien awakened in the soft light of the single lamp to find Taylor sitting on her haunches above him once more. This time there was a small package in her hands.

"You know, I didn't make a sound, didn't touch you at all," she said softly, wonderingly. "But I *willed* you to wake up . . . and you did."

"Mmmm," he murmured into her neck as he pulled her down and close, pretending he didn't see what she held. "You took a shower." He bit her neck lightly. "Now I can't tell where I've been. I may have to start all over."

She shivered in answer, then slowly pulled back, troubled. "O'Brien." No, that wasn't right. She began again. "Sean."

"What is it, honey?" he asked gently, loving the softness of her face.

"When . . . um . . . we were married . . ." She didn't seem to be able to go on. Then she forced herself. "You didn't seem to want—to need me as much as now . . ." Her voice trailed off.

"That's not true, Red," he said after a lengthy silence. "I don't know if you remember"—he looked at her archly—"but the first six months we were together we set a few records." He looked down at her face on his shoulder, stilling the hand that played with the curls on his chest. "God, I love it when you blush." And he leaned to kiss one cheek softly. "But, to resume," he continued, "I guess we just got into a normal routine, love. It's human." Then he gave her a wicked look. "Three times a night isn't."

"But . . ." She began, only she couldn't finish.

"But now?" He finished for her, kissing the fingers curled over his. "Well," he said between kisses, "I'll tell you a little secret, Red." He looked into her eyes with a funny smile. "I've been hoarding for you."

For a minute, she didn't understand, then she didn't believe him. Her brows came together. "You mean . . ." She didn't have the courage to ask if he'd "done without" for an entire year, and she wasn't sure if that was what he meant when he answered, "Exactly." But she wasn't prepared to question any further than she already had. He'd told her what she needed to know.

"Ummm," she said, "I have a present for you."

"I was wondering."

Her left hand came up and placed the small box on his chest. He grabbed it in his right, kissed the top of her head, then sat up to examine it.

"Hmm, brown paper with Chinese markings," said the great Christmas-present guesser.

"No fair guessing," she announced, her hand over his on the package. "This one you have to open."

He pretended to consider, then said graciously, "Well, all right," before he started to tear at the paper.

When he opened the small box, his face was a sweet mixture of surprise and wonder.

"I'm not sure," she said as he fingered the detail of the carving, "but I *think* he's a Chinese god of laughter."

She was staring at him, trying to read whether his pleasure was genuine or for her benefit, when he looked up at her, his eyes soft, and said, "Whether it's true or not, that's how I'll always think of him."

Slowly, deliberately, he placed the figure back in the box and away to the side. Standing, he reached a hand down to her and pulled her up. He headed for the stairs, pulling her arm about his waist as they went up. When they reached the unused, beautifully made bed, he drew away to pull down the spread and fold back the top sheet. Then he picked her up, surprising her again, and, holding her over the bed, looked down at her in innocent puzzlement.

"I only wonder," he announced in a Barrymore whisper, "*how* I'm going to thank you."

"O'Brien!" He couldn't be serious. Not again. "You may have a dire medical condition!" she warned.

He dropped her to the mattress and followed swiftly. "I do, I do." He groaned as he licked at her breast, "The pain is terrific. And you'll be sore tomorrow."

"I know," she answered, pressing against him, "I might be sore for a whole week. . . ."

She found the ballet slippers in her suitcase when she unpacked, and she put them on immediately, missing O'Brien more with every moment. Obviously that was what he had intended, she thought ruefully. There wasn't a muscle in her body that wasn't sore in remembrance of him. She wished him the same, but regret was no part of that wishing.

Well, the sooner she got to work, she thought as she pulled out the portable electric typewriter, the sooner they could be together again.

She looked at the BMW through the front window of the small cabin, thinking how sweet he had been when she'd said she wanted to drive up alone.

"It *would* be easier for me if I had transportation so I could come and go as I pleased," she had said shyly, "but I don't want to deprive you of your car if you need it."

"No," he had answered with a sure shake of his head, "it's more dependable than a rental." He searched his discarded jeans for the keys. "I'd worry," he'd finished simply.

It was after two o'clock Sunday afternoon, she was finally almost on her way, and she wanted nothing so much as to stay and sleep in the arms of her love.

But there was work to be done. And she was determined to prove that her rewriting was worth all the trouble she had stirred up.

"You're sure you won't let me drive you and take a train back?"

The idea was so impractical she almost said yes out of pleasure. "You idiot!" she said instead, throwing her arms around his neck to give him a big kiss. Her bags were in the car waiting below, the typewriter on the back seat with the groceries he'd packed for her.

It was past time for her to leave, but her arms still clung to him. Finally she managed to drag herself from him. "I love you," she threw at him as she turned and ran down the stone steps to the car.

She didn't see him almost follow as he saw her trip on the last stair, or the way his face changed as she settled herself, then started the car.

She was afraid to look back, so she almost missed him waving good-bye from the top step. She was glad she had let herself take one last, long look through the mirror. Glad she had told him she loved him.

"Yea-us," she said to herself. "Now to work!" And work she did. The first day, Sunday, she began in the evening and worked long into the night. Monday she woke at eleven, cursed lightly, then smiled, realizing the reason she had overslept. She grabbed a yogurt (bless O'Brien!) and made for the typewriter. From then on it was heaven. This script was meant for this treatment, she'd felt it, but could hardly contain her pleasure as each character was reshaped, given a chance to express her *exact* idea through the rewrite.

Soon she realized that except for the two major characters, she had given them only vague personalities before, vague characteristics. She had thought it an infringement on the actor to be so specific. But now, she realized, she was actually giving the actors characters of substance to portray, as opposed to the stereotypical maid or butler.

Luckily she could use the character of those already cast to embellish the scenes with eccentricity.

It was going well, very well. She hadn't made a mistake in insisting. O'Brien would love it . . . she hoped. Before she knew it, it was five o'clock Saturday morning and she was hard into the finish of the third act.

In two hours she would be through. Wouldn't O'Brien be surprised to see her back early, all done?

But right now, she needed to bathe more than anything, and she blessed Rhea for the thousandth time for installing plumbing in the isolated cabin.

"Honey?" she heard the voice call. Her head was full of lather, her ears too. It couldn't be . . .

"Oh, there you are," he said with relief from the other side of the shower curtain. Then he swept aside the curtain, letting water drench him and the bathroom floor.

"Rinse your hair, Red. I've already showered." Just like that, she thought to herself. Just like that she smiled her welcome to him.

"Oh, what the hell!" he said as he stepped into the narrow stall and kissed her deeply, warmly, and with hunger as his hands moved in her hair, rinsing out the soap. His jeans and shirt were getting soaked, and were delicious in their friction against her.

"You," she accused in greeting, "are the funniest man I've ever met."

He looked at her, then at his shower attire, and

asked, "I don't suppose you're referring to my ability as a comic."

She couldn't help the giggle that escaped her. "Comedian, yes, comic . . . ? I don't know."

Her hands were slipping through the opening of his western-styled shirt. "You wear this one for me?" she asked as she slowly unsnapped every button-snap with languid, deliberate pleasure.

He pushed her away from him and out of the shower without answering. She grabbed a towel as he followed and began to strip off his wet clothing. By the time he was done, she was before him with another towel, poised and ready.

He stared right into her eyes as he lifted his arms in surrender. When she said, "Turn," he turned. When she said, "Open," he widened the space between his legs, and neither of them said a word until she dropped the towel to the floor and said, in echo of him once again, "C'mere," with her naked arms spread wide to receive him.

He came to her and grabbed her round the waist, lifting her from the ground to walk her to the cozy, unmade double bed.

Once before it, he pushed her gently with his weight onto its surface and held her tightly to him.

"I couldn't stand it another minute," he announced to the top of her head.

"I'm so glad to see you," she answered in perfect accord.

"I almost came up here three times this week." He bit gently at one ear.

Where had her reserved, private, careful man gone to? "Do you know what you do to me when you admit things like that?" she asked him seriously, holding him from her. Some part of her wondered if she wasn't being manipulated very cleverly.

"No . . . does it get to you like you get to me?" His answer was perfect, dissolving her doubts.

"I'm going to do something very stupid," she announced deliberately, hating herself for her horrid sense of timing and insecurity, but still determined.

It took him a minute, hauling himself up on his elbows, above and around her, to ask the appropriate question. "Hmm?"

"I want you to read what I've done. Now."

"I don't care, Red—" he began.

"Sean"—that silenced him—"please."

Infuriatingly he took his time before he finally gave a small nod. But he had something else to say. "I want you to know, Red, that even though you and I are working on this play, even though you wrote it and I am directing it . . . it doesn't mean a damn thing in the larger scheme of things. I don't care if we *are* divorced—to me, you are still my wife. I want you, and I don't care who or what tries to come between us. I know we can make it work. And that's all I have to say."

She couldn't move. Those were the words she had prayed she would hear from him since the moment he'd reappeared on her doorstep. Now she didn't know what to do with them.

And then he said, "So, whether or not I agree with the rewrites, things between us *will* be the same."

But that only kicked up her anger. "Don't be so fast to condemn, bucko! Or"—she couldn't help it, he infuriated her so—"be so sure of your conquest!"

Her eyes were green stone, so he knew he had made a mistake, although he was damned if he knew where. Withdrawing from the bed—that action being the better part of valor, he was sure—he went to the desk, on which there was a neat pile of pages.

Sitting, totally comfortable and without a stitch on, he began to read. In three minutes he had scooped up all the loose pages and returned to the bed a few feet behind him. He ignored Taylor as he plopped down and spread the pages before him. Then, knowing he would be at least forty-five minutes and she would need something to do, he looked up to find her watching him.

"Got any eggs left?" the monster asked. Then he looked at her again. "Just what the hell *have* you been eating?" His glance raked over her, and not approvingly. "My lord, Taylor, you must have lost ten pounds!"

"Nothing like it," she reassured him with slightly bad humor. "Five or six at most," and she pulled on jeans, shirt, and shoes.

"I packed you enough of those frozen gourmet dinners to last *three* weeks!" he bellowed at her. "Didn't you eat at all?"

"No! I starved myself so you'd yell at me like this! Honestly! Big deal, O'Brien! Why don't you just shut up and read the rewrites while I fix breakfast?"

"Fine," he answered, knowing he had overreacted. But Taylor was at actress weight already. She couldn't afford a weight loss. And he had no idea when her last checkup had been.

He forced himself to pay attention to what he read while Taylor slipped on a robe and moved to the other side of the cabin to the kitchen.

She opened the nearly full carton of eggs, dug around in the fridge for accoutrements, and began to cook with ferocity. She beat the eggs to oblivion while she watched O'Brien surreptitiously.

The cabin was so small. And time stretched without end. Finally, despite the fact that she knew he had not finished, she turned and announced, "Ready," and sat at the small breakfast table, a meal she had no desire for in front of her.

He didn't move for a minute or two, making her even more impatient. Then, when he did move, it was with script in hand, his eyes never leaving it.

She glared at him without effect while he ate and read and paid her not the slightest attention. He finished bacon, eggs, and two pieces of toast before turning back to the bed and flopping down upon it again.

Taylor decided it was time for a walk.

Quietly, so that he wouldn't believe she had gone off in a huff—which was exactly what she *was* doing—she let herself out the door. Once into the woods, she forgot her ill-humor and simply absorbed their serenity.

She thought, as she had so many times throughout this last, solitary week, of when O'Brien had told her of his time in the woods a year ago. Their hearts were so in tune: What pleased them, what made them laugh, their understanding of each other, their compassion, their tempers . . . the way they made love.

The fierceness of the way she wanted him frightened her. Nothing was settled yet, and she didn't dare feel this want. And yet she did. It seemed beyond her control, beyond her own volition. Yet her need for his respect for her work vied even with that want. That was why she had interrupted their lovemaking. She was afraid that her love for him would rob her of her self-awareness, her sense of her worth as an artist.

Too, she didn't want him to coddle her because he had just made love to her and had no wish to hurt her. But, dammit, he could have given her some indication of the direction of his opinion. But no, he let her look on and simmer. Infuriating man!

She walked on for another half hour, making her own path through the tangled woods, never too far from the cabin. After she had backtracked for the third time, she decided she had given him long enough to finish.

She also realized that whether he loved or hated her changes, she would survive. And so would their feelings for each other.

She wanted, more than anything, to reassure O'Brien of just that. She made her way back quickly.

Eleven

She found him asleep on his back in the middle of the big bed she had found so empty during the past week.

Moving as quietly as she could, she removed the haphazardly scattered pages from the bed and gave another, longer look at the man before her.

His right forearm was thrown over his eyes in fatigue, his still-nude body was relaxed, legs apart.

Taylor had no idea whether he had finished reading. Neither did she care. She understood, now, that he was right; *they* were what mattered.

Looking at him, so weary, so defenseless, in his deep sleep made her feel a rush of tenderness that combined with her love in a most dismayingly erotic fashion. She spared only a tiny moment of doubt that she should disturb him when he was obviously worn out, before she began to remove her clothes, her eyes never leaving him.

By the time she had finished undressing, her heart was beating double time in excitement. Moving carefully, she maneuvered her way to where he lay so still. For a long time she simply looked at him, and looked her fill before, her pulse running a race once again, she bent to kiss the top of the thigh nearest her.

As if drawn, her soft kisses moved toward his heat, nibbling lightly. Under the first touch of her lips in a gentle kiss against him, he hardened, his eyes flying open. He gave a small start, shoulders rising from the bed, before he realized that Taylor was truly with him, that he was not in the midst of a dream. It was another moment before he realized that he didn't want to move. This was indeed the stuff of dreams.

When she felt him awaken with a jolt, she simply lay her head down on his taut stomach, rubbed her cheek against his skin, and felt his stomach muscles loosen, others tighten. His hand came to rest lightly on her hair.

He felt her breath, the heat of it upon him, driving him, yet he waited. When her tongue flicked at him lightly he was, even so, unprepared for the shock that ran through him, and he gasped in surprise. Unsure of his control and wanting to feel her lips under his, he reached for her shoulders, only to feel her grasp his hips in a firm grip and hold on to him, her lips running lightly over him all the while. He groaned aloud, and she gave a soft, sympathetic laugh before continuing her program.

Not to be outdone, O'Brien twisted down until Taylor was positioned where he was able to retaliate appropriately with his own skills.

The violence of her response sent tremors

through her, so strong that O'Brien pulled from her a moment to gasp, "I love it when you do that!" in a harsh, low whisper, sending another tremor down her body.

They kept pace with each other beautifully, each intent on the other's pleasure, until finally Taylor tore herself away.

"Wait!" Urgently she held out a hand toward him. "Please, Sean, everything's going too fast," she got out between the deep breaths she was pulling hard into her lungs. "I want it to last."

Then he lay beside her, pulling her onto his shoulder, his hand tangled in her wild hair. He wasn't even aware of how possessive his hand was as it splayed to cradle her head, holding her against him.

He glowed with a light sweat that intensified his scent in her nostrils, making them dilate slightly. One of her hands was tangled in the thick fur of his chest.

She was electrically aware of the texture of his skin against hers, the muscles of his thigh, covered with soft black hair that teased her own skin.

"I love you," Sean said, straight into her eyes, his lashes contrasted black against blue, the blue of those deep, magic eyes.

Just as her heart had begun to slow, he sent it pounding once more with those three simple words. She surged against him.

"You were right." She had to make sure he knew. "None of it matters, only us." She leaned up to kiss him, needing the contact.

It was a kiss he would remember long. It said so many things: Communion, commitment, the sweetness of warmth, with just a hint of passion withheld.

"I'm glad, Red, so glad," he said intently, before he bent to thank her with a kiss that no longer withheld anything. The fire it built ran through her in a torrent. She pushed closer to him, but it wasn't enough, she wanted to meld with him through their skin, to become part of him.

When he felt her begin to tremble he gave a low, raw groan and crushed her to him.

"Tay," he groaned, in a voice she didn't recognize, "I need you."

"Ah, love," she answered into the warmth of his neck, "my love." Then his hands were everywhere, sliding over her, leaving heat in little trails behind him.

"Mmmmm," he said into her mouth, then again with vibrant urgency.

She felt his powerful arms flex around her before he rolled her over to lie beneath him on the big bed. He pulled back his head to look into her green eyes, with their gold flecks and long lashes. Her cheeks were crimson with passion and emotion, her skin glowing. He couldn't imagine anything more beautiful.

"Keep your eyes open," he said, smoothing the hair from her forehead with a hand that was far from steady. "I want to see them when I kiss you." Then he bent with his lips parted, reaching for hers.

It was one of the most unique experiences Taylor had ever had. They spoke with their eyes and the touch of their lips at the same time, saying things they never could have said before. His eyes were dark and warm and full of feeling as his mouth made love to her own.

Their dance began.

He set their pace at first. Lying deeply within her, feeling her excited contractions, he began to move with slow and careful effort. Each time he moved, he stretched her, penetrating as deeply as he could, holding her to him with both hands. Then he teased. Taylor arched to capture him again and again, but still he eluded her. Until finally her legs came round him, forcing him into her, as did her hands on his flexing buttocks.

Their rhythm changed, but never faltered, until Taylor gave a wild, sharp cry and stiffened in ecstasy while Sean's fingers moved in slow circles over the soft skin of her back.

He nearly gave in to the fierce compulsion to finish as he felt her orgasm, but he wanted more.

When he felt the tension leave her, he leaned to kiss her lips softly. "You are so beautiful. But when I see what I can do to you, for you, the way you ask me, answer me, you're more lovely than any woman I've ever seen."

Even through the haze of pleasure, with him still hard inside her, Taylor stared. Was this Sean O'Brien, revealing himself, his private thoughts, with tender compliments? She was awed. "Thank you, Sean," she answered simply. "I love you."

"And I love you, Red," he said with his heart in his eyes in a way she had never seen.

His eyes still on hers, he ran his hands up her hips, letting her down slowly until her hips rested on the bed. Still deep within her, he sat back on his legs.

Eyes unwavering, his breath rasping lightly, he let his hands slide lightly up and over her waist. Fingers apart, he tested the silk of her skin, then moved up the sides of her breasts, nipples still

145

hard, to run over her shoulders, her arms, stretching them above her head.

Imprisoning her wrists with his warm hands, he lay above her, not touching except for where they were joined.

Her breath began to shorten as she read his eyes, the wildness, the desire, the love in them. As she needed more and more air her breasts rose, touching his chest with every breath.

He watched her pupils widen and smiled a small smile and lowered his chest the tiniest bit, creating more tantalizing friction.

Then, sensing her readiness, his own eyes darkening, never leaving hers, he began to move.

With each move of his hips, the fur of his chest sandpapered her nipples. It seemed as though her first orgasm had only set her up for this return of excitement.

And this Sean was tender and commanding and vulnerable and sexy all at the same time. She was utterly fascinated, prepared to follow him in any direction.

He was still moving against her with slow, deliberate sweeps when he began to move her hands out, away from her body and downward to lie next to her hips, still in his hard grip.

When he slipped from her, she couldn't help the small cry of disappointment, but she knew he was far from finished. His body, all his muscles, were coiled tight. She could see the light sheen that covered him and knew he was holding back with every ounce of control he had.

"It's okay, love . . ." she said tenderly. "Come to me. I want you."

He gave a one-dimple smile in answer and lifted each of her hands in turn to kiss the palm before he said, "I know, baby, I just want you to want me"—as he paused he sent her a wicked look—"*more*."

As she tried to fathom his words he knelt over her legs and smiled down at her, a gleam in his eye.

"I want you to promise to lie still and let me do what I want." He looked like a little boy with a birthday present. "Please, honey, will you trust me?"

"Of course, Sean." She smiled back. She would have given him anything. They'd never tried whips and chains—she could only hope he wouldn't surprise her now.

Thinking of her pleasure gave him more self-control than times tables or nauseating images ever had, Sean thought to himself in wonder as he gazed down at his love. And beautiful she was, long, slender limbs, with the softest skin, and sweet, sensitive breasts.

He moved to touch her feet, then kissed the arch of each as her toes pointed. He went slowly up her legs, kissing and licking the gooseflesh he created.

At her knees, he became fascinated with shape and form, the cartilage beneath his tongue. Then he covered her thighs with damp kisses, gently nudging her legs apart with his hands at her knees. To her inner thighs he paid special attention, laving the soft skin with his tongue, from her knee to the very top of her thigh. He inhaled deeply with a tense shudder as he passed from one thigh to the other and started all over.

Then he was at her hip with the same loving treatment, and up to her breasts, where he rubbed his face over her again and again before finally taking one nipple into his mouth, then the other. Then he was exploring her other hip.

They were both showing signs of strain when he rested his cheek on her soft stomach as she had done to him, and cuddled her with his face. Then he inhaled deeply again before sliding down between her legs.

All the time Sean had been cat bathing and exploring her, Taylor had felt her excitement rise higher and higher. But she had been determined to exhibit the same kind of control Sean obviously had, knowing that the pleasure would only be that much sweeter for the waiting. The first time he had closed his eyes and inhaled her scent with such straining excitement, she'd wanted to leap at him, to tell him to take her now, now!

She hadn't counted, however, on Sean's knowledge of her body and her responses. As soon as she came too close to the edge, he would change his attack, his rhythm, where he touched her, until she was mindless again, her body writhing, her head tossing. Then at last he came to her, in a slow, sensuous entry that ended with a pounding rhythm she needed more than air. He waited only for her beginning contractions and he let go, riding the incredible sensations for so long that he was left shaken and awed at their ending. They both were.

Twelve

"Never. Never in my life. Sean. I . . . it was . . ."
She was without words.

They lay side by side, both of them with limbs
relaxed, sated, unable to move as yet. At her words,
Sean gathered her close in his arms and gently
kissed her hair.

"For me, too, love."

She lay quietly in his arms, wondering whom
he had been practicing with, wondering if she was
being too suspicious.

Casually she asked, "You been taking lessons,
O'Brien?" Her fingers lay on his chest. She
watched it rise and fall.

He raised her chin with one hand and looked
into her eyes. "Do you believe that, Red?" he asked
carefully.

He had gone right to the heart of her playful

question. She was ashamed. She couldn't bear to dirty what had happened between them.

"No, Sean, I believe what happens between us has always been our own magic. Today we grew a little more." She looked up at him with mischief in her expression. "Even though it *was* incredible." She went on, needing to correct her error. "It's just . . . I suppose . . . I don't really . . . we never really talked about . . ." She swallowed. She was making a mess of this. "Oh, never mind."

"It has suddenly dawned on me"—he turned her face back to his with small kisses—"that my wife is jealous."

She sighed deeply in defeat. Well, wasn't she? But she seized on the words she *could* refute.

"I'm not . . ." But then she stopped, trying to end whatever it was in her that was rebelling against this happiness. She would *not* destroy what they had by being so stupid and rebellious, just because she was afraid to have it taken from her.

"Ah, the lady concedes, despite her better judgment." He kissed her jaw, her cheek, her lips softly, but with a certain sureness. "She *is* jealous and she *is* my wife."

She closed her eyes in humiliation that he would read her so easily.

But he wasn't finished. "Well, I do have a word to say on both issues, but"—he reentwined their legs—"definitely *not* for the press."

"O'Brien—"

"My love, at the risk of having you disbelieve me again, or question my virility—" She squirmed; he couldn't resist teasing her. "I have been faithful to you . . . I never doubted that we would get back together, or that we were still married . . .

although legally . . ." He looked wistful, and she would have told him she'd do anything he wanted, if she'd only been able to speak.

He sensed her trouble as he sensed too much about her, and held her quietly in his arms for a few moments, until she had collected herself enough to say with a stronger voice, "I'm very glad, Sean . . . that there was, is, no one else. Very glad."

"You idiot," he answered fondly.

"Sean, it's never been so . . . so totally consuming for me before. Is that because of what we're feeling now? Or . . . I don't even know what I want to ask you."

"We were married for a while, Red. Are you telling me you weren't involved when we made love?" Maybe he was being prickly, but he did have his pride.

She lay naked in his arms, blushing rose red from her forehead to mid-breast. He couldn't help but appreciate it. But he still waited for her answer.

"O'Brien, you jerk!" Now, *that* startled him from his thoughts! "You can take your macho pride in your expertise and *shove* it!" They were no longer lying close in each other's arms. "You, you dumb donkey, have always been good in bed—to anyone you shared the experience with, I have no doubt! But you, you wretch, have never seemed to give as much of yourself, to reveal so many of your own sacred thoughts." She was quaking with indignation. "To hell with your *bloody* expertise!"

"Bloody?" Why, she wasn't even British, he thought, amused.

"You, you cretin, think that because you manipulated me with your course in refined sexual advances, that I would be bowled over? Ha!" She was standing now, beside the bed, unable to be even within arm's reach of the monster.

"Temper, Red," he warned, still at ease on the bed.

"You're right," she answered as she turned with deliberate calm to yank a khaki jump suit from the small closet and pull it on. But before she had touched the zipper, he was behind her, hand on her hands.

"I think we've played this scene before," he said quietly over her ear. Taylor stiffened at his words, then turned quickly in his arms to bury her face in his hard chest, wrapping her arms about his waist as her lips buried themselves in the thick black hair.

"You arrogant bastard," she whispered to his chest. "I almost did it again . . . Oh, Sean, how will we ever survive?"

"We caught ourselves today," he answered. "It will, like all things, become easier with time." Then he rubbed his chin thoughtfully. "Although we *do* seem to fight more now."

But she jumped right in, as he'd hoped she would. "We're just getting acquainted with the real us." She was triumphant, sure she was right, but she crossed her fingers behind her back just the same.

He pulled her crossed fingers from behind her back and kissed them gently. "Romantic, huh?"

She put her arms around him. "I'm sorry I called you a bastard. You're not."

"Oh," he said, "does that mean I'm still a—what was it now—oh, yes, a donkey?"

Still unwilling to face those eyes, Taylor spoke wryly to a collarbone. "I wish you hadn't asked that." Then, having punished him enough, she put her arms high around his neck and rested her head, rubbing softly on his chest.

"I don't know what came over me, Sean. I just felt so vulnerable and . . . stirred up. Making love with you has always been wonderful, so special and full. But"—finally she could look up into his eyes—"I just never felt so close, so in tune with anyone in my life." She stepped lightly on his toes so she could reach his lips with a light kiss that was almost a benediction. "I think I got scared." She shook her head and lifted her brows. "No control."

"It was an incredible gift, Red," he answered simply, telling her with his expression how deeply he was affected. Then he bent to lick at her ear and whispered, "Be scared *with* me."

O'Brien awoke to the sound of a typewriter. He propped himself up on one elbow as he followed the line of the long black cord that trailed to the door and out to the front porch.

Smiling, he flopped over on his back and gave an immensely satisfying, spine-straightening stretch before he relaxed once more.

God, he had everything now, he thought to himself. He wondered how Taylor felt about kids. He'd never really thought about them before, but suddenly the picture of his Red with a babe at her breast came to his mind. Hmm, he'd have to consider that one.

Turning to the clock on the night table, he saw that it was late afternoon. What he wanted now was coffee.

Taylor hadn't slept at all. She was too restless from the hodgepodge of emotions that pulled at her. There was a lot she wanted to think about.

It had happened again, that loss of control in combination with incredible pleasure.

After O'Brien fell asleep in her arms, she held him for some time, reveling in their new, special closeness. Then she needed to move.

Sitting on the porch, staring into the leafy greenness all around her, she tried to analyze her behavior of late. She had always had a temper. But suddenly she seemed to be so defensive that she bordered on the hysterical.

It was not a picture she relished. It was much too reminiscent of the child who had run away from her marriage in a tantrum.

And she thought she had grown up more in this last year.

There was no doubt about it. She had left O'Brien, he hadn't left her. He had come back to patch things up. She had simply run. Adults, she told herself sternly, do not run because they're afraid to be left. They trust. They cope. And you, my girl, are going to start learning how to be an adult!

Feeling relieved, and, yes, loved, Taylor decided to put this hopeful energy to work, and went inside to collect the typewriter and original script. Whether O'Brien liked the changes or not, she needed to finish them.

Once inside the cabin, she wasted a moment or two staring in ridiculous, glorious fascination at "O'Brien Asleep" before she filed the picture away in her box of memories and got to the business at hand.

After two and a half hours, Taylor gazed fixedly at the last page in her hands, wondering if it worked. She had taken both endings, first having things *seem* to be resolved, with the lovers resigned to their "fate," then having them both become angered at their very resignation. The play would end romantically, with a fight, both lovers explaining at the top of their lungs that they would make their own way, their own "fate," and damn all who tried to stop them. They would be giving each other exactly the same arguments and ultimatums, each ignoring the other's case completely, as the curtain came down in a rush.

O'Brien watched from the doorway, a mug of coffee in each hand, as Taylor finally smiled a wide, delighted smile and murmured to herself, "Yes, yes, yes!" Then she said, "O'Brien," and whirled around and to her feet in one smooth motion.

Finding him before her, she was—absurd, but true—suddenly shy. "I, uh, was just coming to wake you."

"So I heard." He was laughing at her again, without a change of expression, but she could tell by the eyes.

Composing herself, she looked at his hands. "Mmm, coffee, perfect." Then she couldn't restrain herself any longer. "I think I've got the ending. But I want you to pick up from where you left off. Okay?" She could hardly contain her impatience, and when O'Brien had said, "Fine," and gone to the steps to sit, she gave him the finished pages.

Refusing even to pretend indifference, she sat beside him, sipped her coffee and stared at his face until he looked up at her for the third time and said, "Can I do somethin' for you, lady?" with one raised brow.

"Okay, okay . . ." she grumbled, and went inside to start dinner.

Glaring at the clock, she estimated that he would take about twenty minutes. Finally feeling the fatigue of working all night and making love nearly the whole day, she pulled two mismatched frozen dinners from the freezer without looking, turned on the oven, and pushed them in. After that, she changed into an oversized football jersey of O'Brien's that she had confiscated long ago, and crawled into the still-mussed bed. Smiling as she smelled O'Brien on the pillow, she snuggled down and fell asleep almost instantly.

Forty minutes later, Sean entered the house. He smelled dinner cooking as he came through the door, then he saw her asleep amid the tumbled covers. He'd let her sleep another hour or so before waking her to eat. Knowing her work habits, she would probably need to go right back to sleep after she'd eaten. He turned the oven to warm.

He found a pencil, gathered up the rest of the script, and settled himself in the big wing chair near the fireplace to make directorial notes on the major changes. Her instincts had been right, perfect, from beginning to end. This play *could* become a classic comedy. It would certainly be a Broadway success.

He paused a moment to give Taylor a glance, but her breathing was still slow and steady.

He was filled with pride in her work. And he was even more certain than he had been a year ago that this was movie material.

He had only to explain that and his actions to Taylor.

He didn't think of himself as a particularly courageous or particularly cowardly man. But the idea of facing Taylor with an explanation of his legal actions gave him a distinct sense of foreboding. Damn. He just couldn't afford to shake the growing sense of trust between them. Well, he thought, he would just have to hope a time would arise when he would be able to explain naturally.

Right now, it was past time for dinner.

Taylor woke to the sound of O'Brien's voice quoting from nonexistent reviews for a play not yet staged. "Taylor Neal O'Brien is Broadway's newest shining star. . . . *The Run of the Play* is a stunning night in the theater . . . Boffo, smasho, zippo, Do da . . ."

"Do da?" Taylor laughed.

"So . . ." O'Brien shrugged as he gathered her in his arms for a cradling hug. "Write your own reviews." He looked deep into her eyes and said with feeling, "Soup's on."

"Yes." She spread wide her arms, and addressed the nation at large. "The man has unswerving dedication to his art—that is, after sex and food. Hopefully in that order."

"Irreverent," he disclaimed in snide disgust.

"*Do* da!" she answered.

Thirteen

After dinner, Taylor asked O'Brien how he had gotten to the cabin, widening her eyes only slightly when he answered, "I gave a cabbie a hundred."

"You wanna go back tonight?" she asked, not knowing what plans he had made.

"I would love to stay here and relax another day, but I want to work on 'the changes,' " as they had dubbed her rewrites.

Taylor nodded. "I'm about ready for some city noise, anyway." She didn't really care where they were, as long as they were together. She felt like she had when they had first fallen in love, girlish and happy and needy of his company.

She slept through the entire drive back to the city, only waking when he kissed her cheek and said, "Home, love."

O'Brien had found a parking place almost in front of their brownstone and had carried everything inside except Taylor. When she couldn't seem to open her eyes, he carried her too. By the time he had topped the inside staircase, he was breathing heavily. "Some hero," he muttered to himself, and was glad Taylor wasn't awake to tease him.

He returned downstairs after placing her atop the coverlet, and put away the groceries before carrying her small bag upstairs.

Once upstairs, O'Brien turned on a radio station that played soft jazz and went to the bed with the intention of removing Taylor's clothes. He felt a bit like a dirty old man as he tugged the jump suit from her for the second time that day. Then he could only stare and laugh. Only Red would put on a regulation khaki flight suit over French lingerie. He smiled and put a hand on each hip to tug at the small satin bows. Then he unbuttoned each of the tiny peach satin buttons of the low-cut silk chemise.

He couldn't resist just one swipe down over her equally silky skin before he placed a hand in the small of her back and lifted her to remove the bits of unnecessary covering.

As he lay her back down on the coverlet, she squirmed and murmured, "Come to bed, Sean." He blinked, and wondered briefly if she had really been asleep at all, but then she said, "I missed you," in a voice that trailed away. And after that, he only wanted to hold her.

He undressed hurriedly, wondering if he had locked the front door, and pulled down the covers beneath Taylor, only to cover them both as soon as he had her in his arms.

Feeling happier than ever in his memory, Sean kissed the top of that red head and slept.

This time it was Sean who awoke first, and, noting the depth of her sleep, decided Taylor had not yet made up for what she had missed during the past week. Anyway, it was still early. And *he* couldn't wait to get to work.

All the time he worked on his notes for the stage play, O'Brien kept visualizing how much more *The Run* would come to life on the screen, the depth he would be able to add to the characterizations without dialogue. Terrific, it was going to be terrific. He would tell her this week, after she had had a chance to see the changes on the stage. Slow and easy, that was the ticket . . . but it was getting harder.

Soon he heard Taylor singing in the shower. He had to laugh. She was singing "My Funny Valentine," and he knew it was for himself.

She found him in the study before she went out. She was dressed in a red Yankees T-shirt and white nylon shorts with the oldest, dirtiest pair of running shoes he had ever seen. As she came into the room, both her hands were occupied in fixing her high ponytail.

When he looked up from his notes, his eyes returned again and again to her Yankees emblem. "Aren't you gonna wear a running bra . . . or something?" he asked stupidly.

"Good morning to you too! And I *am* wearing a running bra!"

"Hmm." He rose, walked over to her, and placed one hand over her breast, his fingers lightly tracing. "I couldn't tell." His eyes had a rapt expression.

"Unless you intend to make pancakes with this batter," she teased him, "I am going to take my sauce and go run."

"Good morning," he said with a sheepish grin and rosy complexion. "I'm working," he added thickly, as if waiting to be praised.

Taylor couldn't, couldn't even try, to resist. She simply patted his head like a good pup and said, "And a *very* good boy you are, too," before turning to go. At the doorway, she "noticed" that her shoelace was untied and bent to retie it, glancing back at O'Brien. However, when he growled, "If you don't get going, you might just get what you're asking for," she let out a little shriek and ran down the stairs and out of the house without a backward glance.

Upon her return, he was waiting—the sneak!—behind the front door to grab her, even though she screamed *very* loudly, and to push her into an already running shower. He *had* had the foresight to remove his own clothes. There he removed her sopping clothes and made her a dress out of shaving cream. And when she complained of the scent—of course, courtesy demanded that she let him complete his creation first—he began again with her perfumed guest soap. Uhmmm, it was a very nice morning.

By the afternoon, they were down to the serious wrangling over scene staging. Except, of course, when they were interrupted by all those telephone calls for Taylor. She responded to each with: "Fine . . . fine . . . oh, yes, just fine . . ." O'Brien managed to control his annoyance through Rhea, O'Malley, and Taylor's mother, but when it happened with one of the production assistants, his patience began to wear a little thin. He waited until she got off the line. Then he said in a steady voice, "Will you please either take the damn thing off the hook or give them all the sterling details?"

But his one and only love just smiled and turned back to work. She knew it was wicked, but she did so love it when she got to him.

That night they simply slept in each other's arms. No "sorry, not tonight" or "hmm, I'm exhausted," just a gentle kiss, a sigh, and a bit of cuddling.

O'Brien brought her coffee in the morning along with a warning. "Twenty minutes, Red. The alarm didn't go off, and the director's a stickler for punctuality."

Well, so much for cuddling and kisses, she realized. She went to rehearsal in moisturizer, a leotard, shorts, and her glowing good health, but she was on time, damn his eyes! Aaand, she fixed the image up in the "ladies" once she was there—so there, O'Brien!

O'Brien had left home before her to make copies of the new script, but he was already at the long meeting table as she left the bathroom. Scripts were being passed around and chairs commandeered.

O'Brien held the back of the chair on his right and nodded to her obliquely. When she had seated herself, he placed his right foot upon the seat of his own chair and leaned forward to rest his elbow on that knee.

Without a word, he had taken command and quieted the company. She had to present him with a small look of admiration, which he refused—upon his dignity, no doubt—to acknowledge.

"Ladies and gentlemen," he began easily, "you will see before you"—here he paused for suspense—"a few minor changes in the script."

The groans were deafening. They died away as Sean raised one hand.

"I don't think you'll mind too much when you see how the characters have been highlighted . . . and"—he strove to make himself heard over the sudden rustlings—"that is a debt we all owe to the writer and leading lady. The reading starts now." His voice rose in volume and dimension. "Act one, scene one!"

The reading went well. It went beautifully.

By the time they broke for lunch, most of the actors had a firm grasp on the characterizations Taylor had tried to convey. Some immediately, some with slow, surprised comprehension. By one o'clock Sean called a halt with the words: "Getting somewhere!" Then he waved a hand at them and smiled in royal acknowledgment. "Be back at two"—his eyes narrowed—"on the dot!"

When everyone had determined what and where for lunch, Sean called for Taylor from the wings. She had almost agreed to go for a hamburger, but when O'Brien called, she realized he hadn't made plans for a business lunch and went toward him eagerly.

As she came close, he merely turned a stern face to her and pointed to her dressing room with one long finger.

Frowning slightly, Taylor followed his steps and tried to jog her memory for what she might have done now. But try as she might, she couldn't imagine what might be her latest.

Her brows were still drawn in concentration when she heard the door close and the lock click behind her. As she looked up, O'Brien swooped. She spent a moment wondering what had brought on this intense surge of passion before she gave up.

All the time he was kissing her, he was moving her to the couch against the wall, until he had pressed her down onto it. She didn't really feel the necessity to protest until she suddenly had a thought.

"O'Brien, these walls are like paper," she warned up into his dark unfocused eyes.

"Then," he answered between kisses, refusing to quibble, "we'll just have to be very, very quiet. . . ." And, so saying, he smothered the giggle she almost let escape.

Afterward, lying there in his arms, she snuggled into one shoulder and complimented, "Much nicer than yogurt, O'Brien."

"Mmmm, but we've got that, too," he said as he waved at the dressing table and a brown paper bag she hadn't noticed before.

Then, gentleman that he was, he heaved his great length up and returned with the "goods" and two Kleenex for napkins.

They fed each other yogurt sitting in the buff on that ancient couch. O'Brien was remarkably clumsy, but he always cleaned up his spills.

"Actually, Red," he said with the last of the yogurt, "I just wanted to get you alone to tell you how proud I am of you, even for standing up to me, and how well the changes fit the scheme of the show." She was a statue with an O for a mouth. "But," he continued, enjoying her stunned expression, "when you attacked me"—he went on over the sputtering noises—"I just couldn't resist." He ignored her—a mistake—as he pulled on jeans and shirt. She began to dress, too, quiet as she slipped easily into her clothes, letting the tension build without the aid of any facial expression. When she was dressed, she went to the lighted mirror, pulled her hair back into her ponytail, and tossed back over her shoulder, "You realize, of course, Mr. O'Brien, that if you don't pay me the fifty dollars, I'll have to file suit for sexual harassment?"

He came up behind her, massaging her shoulders lightly, and looked into the mirror with a tender expression. Then he tucked a hundred-dollar bill down the front of her leotard.

Her eyes flew to his. Surely he couldn't mean, didn't he realize she was only . . .?

"That, my one and only, is for you to buy a bra to wear under your leotard . . . so that you don't waste rehearsal hours driving me out of my mind."

She relaxed. "Well, O'Brien, if you really don't feel up to it." It took him less than three seconds to retaliate with a kiss that drew her upright and against him, leaving her in no doubt whatsoever of his interest or his energy.

Suddenly he dropped her back onto the chair. "Well . . . gotta go." And he went to the door, unlocked it, and started out. But while his hand was still on it she called, "Ohhhhh-Brien?" and—sucker that he was—he turned, only to have his innocent expression wiped neatly away, compliments of a small, but hard foam-rubber pillow, thrown by an expert hand, if she did say so herself!

Her laughter could be heard halfway across the empty stage, and it only intensified as O'Brien tested his nose and lisped, head thrown back for his exit, "Zank Gott, she didn't ruink my profeeel!" A moment later she could hear him bellowing center stage, "To work!"

Whoops, no privileged character she. And so she ran.

• • •

Rehearsals, long or short, were a pleasure for Taylor. Her talents were being utilized, she was starring in her brainchild, working with a director she respected. It felt good, all of it.

"Dammit, Red, it's stale! I don't believe you."

"*You* the director, or *you* in the mind of the character, O'Brien? He's not supposed to believe me—I'm lying, for God's sake, and we both know it."

"So you're lying. Why? What's your reasoning? What are you afraid of? What's your purpose? I don't see any of that."

They were standing downstage with two feet between them, yelling at the top of their lungs, totally unaware of how their argument relieved and entertained the rest of the cast and crew. The shoe had finally fallen.

"Life, I want to see life! This is no time to pull back and enjoy your accomplishment!"

Damn him!

"You have a job to do here, and I want to see everything you've got." He ignored her rigid stance and indignant face and turned. "Let's go."

That night Taylor didn't wait for O'Brien to be ready before she left the theater. She left as soon as she could and began walking uptown. It was rush hour, but Taylor didn't even look for a cab. She walked uptown and crossed streets until she came to Central Park. There she made her way to the east side until she came upon the small pond where children always sailed boats in good weather. She sat on the hill above it.

She knew he was right. So why didn't that make everything fine? After a month and a half of rehearsals, some things were bound to go stale. It happened to everyone. And, she acknowledged, she didn't begrudge O'Brien the right, the necessity, to call her on it. He didn't speak to her any differently than he did to anyone else, did he? Well, maybe he was a bit more stringent with her. So what? She could take it, couldn't she? And the answer came back to her immediately. Yes, she could take it. But she didn't want to have to take it home.

Finally she breathed a long sigh of relief. Show business was an ego-lifting, ego-smashing business. Still, Taylor felt safe in her crazy world as long as she could analyze and approve of her feelings as natural or justified.

Now that she knew why she still resented O'Brien, she felt much better.

If he were another director, she would have tucked away the memory of today's rehearsal and thought about it later. If she had agreed or disagreed she would still have tried to do things his way first. And she would have gone home to another situation and complained about rehearsal. But as long as O'Brien and she worked together, half of her rooting team had to be on the other side. It was tough sometimes. Well, she could handle it.

He was waiting for her when she walked in, standing against the big windows with his hands in his back pockets.

She walked around the couch and plopped down on it. Then she looked up at him. His eyes showed nothing.

"I'm not mad, Sean," she said finally. "But I'm not real excited about fighting with the director and then coming home to him either."

Startled by her honesty, the depth of it, he blinked. Then he said, "So you want some time alone?" He would understand if she did—everyone did sometimes.

"Well, that depends," she began, and he started to relax as he saw the gleam come to her eye. "Can Sean come out to play?"

"Just what did you have in mind?" he asked, raising one eyebrow.

"*One Hundred and One Dalmatians* is playing at the Regency. Or we could go uptown and listen to some jazz."

"Disney?" His face was transformed, animation the key. "What time's the show?"

"Well"—she drew it out as long as possible—"there's one at nine-thirty."

"Great!" Then he was pulling her off the couch and toward the door. "Come on. I'll buy you a pizza at Ray's."

"Pizza!" She groaned. "Salad?" she countered hopefully.

"Hot dog?"

"Hot dog! O'Brien, do you know what the FDA's rat-hair allowance is per hot dog?"

"You know," he said, pulling her behind him to the Seventh Avenue subway stop, "you have the most depressing way of getting your own way. Rat hair?"

"Thirty for each hot dog," she said with smug satisfaction, much to the disgust of O'Brien and the lady standing in line next to them.

But they didn't bother her a bit. She hated hot dogs.

Fourteen

The day of dress rehearsal Taylor tried to be away from the house and keep busy.

While Sean spent the day at the theater, solving a thousand last-minute problems, Taylor went to the Met, had lunch with Rhea, saw an afternoon movie, and then, reluctantly, went home.

She debated doing the ironing, but, afraid of the results in her present mood, restrained herself.

It was five o'clock. She was to be at the theater at seven. There was nothing on earth that could make her eat dinner, so what to do?

She was in this highly nervous state when the phone rang.

"Hello?" she answered, cheering at the reprieve.

"Hello, is Sean there?" came a middle-aged male voice.

"No, I'm sorry. Would you like to leave a message?"

"Oh. Well, no. I just wanted to wish him the best for tomorrow night, and to tell him that the studio is ready to go ahead any time with production. Oh, this is Jo Barbutti."

"Production, Mr. Barbutti?" She was mystified.

"Yeah, on *The Run of the Play*. Is this Sean's secretary?"

Calm. She was perfectly calm.

"No. But I'll make sure he gets your message, Mr. Barbutti." Then she hung up.

She knew O'Brien was due home any minute, but she couldn't wait. She dialed O'Malley's number.

"O'Malley!" she began without ceremony when she heard his voice. "What do you know about a Jo Barbutti and his interest in *The Run*?"

There was utter silence.

"O'Malley?"

"I told Sean to stop stalling and tell you, Taylor." He sounded weary. She didn't like it.

"Tell me what?" she asked shortly, steel in her voice. She sensed his hesitation and felt that he was trying to find some way of putting her off.

"Don't do this to me, O'Malley. You're my legal representative. I have a right to know what's going on."

"It's very complicated, involved, Taylor."

"Are you afraid I won't understand the language, O'Malley?" He'd never heard her voice like this.

She could almost see his huge eyebrows meeting in concentration. What the hell was going on?

"Of course not, Taylor. I just think this is something you and O'Brien should discuss in private."

"Oh, we will, O'Malley. And then perhaps you'll tell me why you know all about this—and I somehow get the feeling that you do—and *I* don't." She replaced the phone with a businesslike click.

She began pacing, trying to find a coherent thought in the middle of this jumble. Then she pulled herself up and went to sit on the couch and await O'Brien.

She knew deep in her heart that O'Malley would never willingly betray her or do her out of monies rightly hers. She hadn't signed any new contracts. So what could be going on?

O'Brien walked in. "Hi, hon." He threw his jacket on a chair and went into the kitchen. A moment later he was back with an iced tea, combing one hand through his hair. "I *think* we'll be okay." He smiled tiredly, and held up a thumb. "A carpenter I'm not." He looked at her closely when he noticed the unnatural silence. "Red, you okay?"

"You got a phone call today. Jo Barbutti," she said in a voice that sounded like someone else's. "He said to wish you the best and tell you that the studio is ready to go into production on *The Run* whenever you are."

"Oh, Lord."

"I talked to O'Malley, but he seemed to think that this was something you and I should discuss." Then she stared right into his eyes. "What do *you* think?"

"Oh, Lord," he said again. "I don't blame you for being mad, Red. But I was just waiting for the right time to tell you." He made a face and rested his elbows on his knees before he gave her a measuring look. "Uhm, just what did O'Malley tell you?"

She shook her head slowly, her eyes on him

like a hawk's, and said, "Suppose you just tell me what you're afraid he might have told me."

"Uh, yeah." He looked at his watch. "You know, Red, we really don't have time to get into this right now. Curtain's at eight."

"Just start me on the right track, O'Brien. We can finish up after rehearsal. Suppose you start with Jo Barbutti."

He cleared his throat, took a deep breath. "Jo was the producer on my last picture. I had spoken to him about *The Run* when we were in England." He waited. He knew it was coming. This was all much harder than he had ever imagined it would be.

"You didn't have anything to do with *The Run* when you were in England." Her eyes, that sparkling green, had taken on a dull sheen.

"That's not exactly true, Red. About six months ago I was contacted by one of our backers. He wanted to know if I knew anyone who wanted to take up his investment in *The Run*. It seemed a perfect opportunity for contacting you when the film was done. I jumped at it. Then, when I heard Jo was looking for a new script, I—it just felt right." Why was he so nervous? he wondered. He hadn't done anything wrong except not tell her.

"You expect me to believe that you invested one hundred and seventy five thousand dollars so that you could have another chance with me?" Her voice was soft. He had a feeling he wasn't at his most credible.

"I also believed in the play. And I gave O'Malley an option to find someone to buy me out if it didn't work out between us."

"A written option?" she asked quickly. At this

point, the look he turned on her went right through her without touching her.

"O'Malley and I don't need paper."

"How did you get him to agree?"

"I told him we still loved each other."

"I see."

"Do you?" He was disbelieving.

"Of course, there is another possibility." Still cool, still calm, she went on, "It's possible you made a deal with Mr. Barbutti and came back to insure it."

"I was afraid you might think that. But I never really believed you would." His voice was dead-sounding, flat. Sad.

"I don't know what I believe." She stood and went to the window, wrapping her arms about herself. "Why didn't you tell me before?" When he didn't answer, she turned to find him standing behind her.

"I was waiting for a time when I thought you wouldn't react"—he paused—"like this.

"We have to get to the theater, Taylor," he said firmly. "I know you're thinking the worst of me just now. But we've got so much. Just remember this, too." And though she began to back away from him when she realized his intention, he merely tightened his hold on her and pulled her to him.

She was sure she would feel nothing when he kissed her. But when his lips touched hers so gently, so coaxingly, she felt his own desire withheld until she could meet him halfway. And when she did, his tongue, his lips and teeth set a fire in her that wiped her mind of everything but her love for him and her need for his fierceness, his warmth.

That kiss frightened the hell out of her.

In the midst of it his hand had gone to her

breast. As he pulled away, it was their last contact. He leaned forward a moment to cup it more fully, then reluctantly let her go. "You remember that, and that I love you." He cupped her cheek with one hand. "And I'll take my chances with the rest."

She blinked up at him. Who wouldn't believe this man?

"Time, Red," he said from the door as she stood, still bemused, by the window.

Then she moved fast: Upstairs to grab her makeup case, downstairs to find her shoes . . . under the chair, and her purse near the door.

Then she was facing the big man at the door, and she motioned him onward, knowing he had been enjoying the show, and out they went.

"Dress" was a catastrophe. Everything that could go wrong, did. In the theater, this is known as a good sign. To a playwright, and to many actors, it signals impending doom.

By the end of the rehearsal, Taylor's nerves were a wreck. She had tried to do a professional job, but was still unsatisfied with her performance. When it came time for after-rehearsal notes from O'Brien, she found that he agreed.

"Taylor. I need more from you all round. You can do it. Concentrate, love."

Any other director would have been satisfied with what she had given to the show that night. Not so O'Brien. He knew she was holding back. But the trouble with dress rehearsal is that it is always *only* a rehearsal. Now, a performance . . . She knew she would come alive then, as would everyone else. Although she *did* wish she hadn't given her director cause for complaint.

Funny how she didn't mind anything he said

when he finished it with that endearment, "love."
Better never let him find *that* out.

She waited for him until after twelve. She
knew he had seen her go to her dressing room, so
she wasn't surprised when he appeared in her
open doorway, a lumbering, uncertain bear.

He stared at her as if he could read every
thought, before he held out his hand for her and
said, "Let's go."

It took her less time than a slow cannonball to
meet that hand. Subtle, girl, she told herself. But
she had made her choice.

She had spent an hour waiting for him to wind
up his business. During that time she had decided
to take the final step in her master plan to grow up.
She would trust. Following her instincts, throwing
caution aside, she would trust without further
explanation, without protestations or proof. If she
got hurt, well, it would be just too damn bad. However, she was not willing to put either O'Brien or
herself through any more of this. That is, if she
hadn't already turned him away with her doubts.

So she grabbed his hand with a bit more
enthusiasm than was politic, considering the status of their argument. Although she did manage to
keep the smile she felt inside under wraps.

She would wait until the proper moment. That
moment arrived some five minutes later. In a
checker cab, at a red light, she attacked him—but
with subtlety.

When the light turned red, she leaned across
the wide seat, up inches to bite an earlobe, before
she twisted, settling herself in his lap. He looked at
her as if she were from another planet while his
arms closed around her reflexively.

"So how big a part are we talking about?" she

asked for the driver's benefit as she traced his ear with her lips and tongue.

"Red!" he protested as he tried to reroute a stray hand, aware of the cabbie's interest.

"Come on, lover," she went on as she wiggled her hips slightly. "Tell me." But she had pushed just a tad too far.

Suddenly she was grabbed by the waist and placed back upon the seat. O'Brien leaned his full weight on her for control and spat out, "Baby, I'm gonna give you the starring part if you come across good for me tonight." Her wrists were in his hands. The man was writing this script as he went along. "So show me what you can do, baby." And, just as she looked up at him in admiration, he assaulted her with a vile, perfect kiss to which she could not help but respond—much to the enjoyment of the audience in the front seat.

That was the fastest ride downtown that she could ever recall. Though whether it was the speed of the ride or her preoccupation, she could never decide.

When they did arrive at Bank Street, the driver simply watched with enjoyment as Taylor was hauled out of his cab and into a fireman's carry over the tall man's shoulder, and then he said, "Do you think I could have the lady's autograph, sir?" This she gave, still from the tyrant's shoulder, amazed that she could be recognized though she was still un-movie'd, un-TV'd.

Then O'Brien carried her up the stairs. When he reached the couch in the dark living room he let her stand on her own. But she did a truly terrible weak-kneed faint, so that he grabbed her close before she could fall.

"That's one you're going to have to practice,

Red," he said down into her fluttering eyelashes. "*Not* your most convincing."

"So," she answered as her hands moved lightly over the strongly defined muscles in the arms that held her, "why don't we work on what I *am* good at?"

He stared at her, though he couldn't read her expression in the dark. Then, still holding one arm, he moved with her to the stairs. "Let's go upstairs, where there's some light."

She moved with him easily, and tried not to think about how much she wanted him. His warm, sea scent was teasing her, and she kept thinking of how he had immediately surged against her in the taxi. Clear head, keep a clear head.

Once upstairs he pulled her, not into the bedroom, but into the study. There he pushed her to sit on the sofa before he leaned his own weight against the desk behind him.

She put her feet up under her and tried to appear comfortable under his steady gaze, before he finally said, "Tell me."

"You sure you wouldn't rather discuss this in the morning?" she asked hopefully, knowing her own preference very well.

"Tell me," he commanded.

But she wasn't willing to let things go entirely his way. "Okay. If you come to the bedroom and hold me while I do it."

"*Red*," he warned.

"Please?" And she dropped all pretense. She let him read in her eyes that she needed his love and reassurance in order for her to be able to say the things she wanted him to hear.

Without another word he straightened and held out his hand for her. When she took it he gave her one warm, crushing hug, and gently released her. Then, without ever looking up at him, she tugged him after her into the bedroom.

When they were settled comfortably, leaning against the pillows and headboard, Taylor began simply. "I love you."

His arms tightened around her, and she fit her cheek in the crook of his shoulder and felt such peace. After a few moments, he pulled back a bit and said, "*But . . . And . . .?*"

"That's all. It covers all the territory!" She looked into his eyes and saw such sweetness there, she nearly forgot to finish what she was saying. "I trust you, O'Brien. I know when you do explain, I'll believe you. And I need you to know that, for some reason."

He didn't move for some time, not a muscle, not an eye. Then, so quietly, he said, "Thank you, love." And he leaned to rub his cheek on hers. "Now I want to explain." She was stopped in her protest by one finger against her lips. "No, you gave me the gift of your trust. I want to give you something in return."

If she looked at him, she knew she would cry, so she didn't look, but stared at the open button on the soft denim shirt he wore, and waited for him to continue.

"I've spent a lot of the last year being angry at you for giving up on us so easily and at myself for letting you. The other part of my time has been spent trying to find a way back into our life together." He gave her a small squeeze and went on. "When that backer came to me, it seemed like a godsend, so I mortgaged some property I had in California and bought out the backer. I was scared to death you would see me and start screaming or something. But I needed you too badly." She burrowed further into his arms. "When I first saw you, I knew it would be all right if I could just give you some time. I could see you still loved me. And," he went on wickedly, "it was certainly clear that you still wanted me." She was making small strangled sounds into his shoulder. "When we finally made love, I knew for sure. And it's only gotten better, Red." His chin rested on her head now. "I think we've both grown a lot this last year. But I don't want to be without you anymore. That okay with you?"

"Yes, please," she said against the skin of his neck.

"There's something else, Red." Why did that make her heart leap? "When we got married before, well, I wanted it because, having finally found you, I was afraid to lose you. But I lost you anyway. I think that now, if we work at it, we have something more important. I don't want you because I'm afraid of life without you, but I do want to share my life with you. My life is richer with you." He lifted her chin with one hand. "Red, will you marry me?"

Her eyes filled—oh, stupid reflex—and her throat tightened. When she could finally force words past the tightness there, she said, "O'Brien, you give the damnedest speech!"

"Say yes," he commanded, kissing the very corner of her mouth.

"Hmm?" she answered absently, somehow preoccupied.

"*Say* yes," he said again, trailing soft kisses down her throat to test the silken skin there. Meanwhile one hand had gone exploring in the lower regions.

"That's blackmail," she accused in breathless accents, her own hands moving restlessly.

"Say *yes*."

Well, he *was* persistent. "What about California, your movies?" She'd better get the answers she needed, she was slipping fast.

"Some time here, some time there. And I want to direct you in *The Run*." Then he stopped all contact, though her clothes were half off, and leaned back away from her to pin her with a serious blue gaze. Five seconds, ten, she lost track. "Say *yes*."

"Yes," she answered. "Yes, yes, yes, yes, in every language and in every way, yes. Yes." And when she held out her arms, her love made haste to fill them.

This time there was no thought of male-female or a need for fulfillment. This time she wanted to be a part of him, to be as close to him as possible. This was a celebration.

Her mind was clouded, full of emotion. She didn't really know where or how he touched her or she him. But it was wonderful, it was magic. They weren't terribly creative. They were terribly basic. Their passion for each other carried them. And when her pleasure was the most intense he cried out, "Wait for me, wait!" and followed close behind.

When it was over he held her tightly as she cried in awe and whispered, "It was so beautiful. Oh, Sean."

And the hug he gave her was fierce, before he said again, "I love you, Red, so much."

Then they slept in each other's arms like two babes.

Fifteen

The next morning Taylor woke late. Well, the second time she woke late.

Her eyes had first opened with the dawn. And her errant sense of humor had decided to time O'Brien's reflexive responses. But she wasn't quite sure what the time factor was because of her suspicion that he was awake far in advance of the time when he opened his eyes. Oh, well, she'd just have to try again another time.

When she did awaken a second time, she found a paper heart on the pillow next to her.

It was a childishly romantic thing to do. He had cut it out of newspaper, making it even more ridiculous, and more romantic, and Taylor knew she would hide it away and cherish it always.

Cradling it carefully in her hands, she went to find a place for it in her jewelry box, where she could see it every day.

Too full of everything to face anyone just yet, Taylor showered leisurely and dressed slowly before she made her way downstairs, to find O'Brien lost amid a pile of scripts on the floor of the living room.

At the sound of her step on the stairs he turned to look up at her, and her steps slowed as she took in the picture.

"Hi," she said softly.

"Hi," he said back.

They smiled.

Secrets.

"What are you doin'?" She came down the last of the stairs and sat on the floor beside him.

"Checking out new scripts. There're a couple I'd like to hear your opinion on." The casualness of the words was belied by the intensity between them.

"Mmm. I'd love to," she answered as she lifted one of the manuscripts nearest her. Still looking at the page before her she said, "Thank you for the note." She turned a page.

"Welcome," he answered, just as easily.

They both looked up. Smiled.

No secrets.

The rest of the day passed without their really acknowledging the tension of opening night. Without words they had agreed not to speak of the tensions, the anxieties, it created. They both strove just to relax and enjoy the day.

They went for a long walk and fed the pigeons popcorn in Washington Square Park. They bought ice cream cones and listened to the steel drum players there. Then, holding hands, they walked back home.

O'Brien insisted Taylor take "just a little nap,"

and Taylor agreed on the condition that he take it with her, and O'Brien agreed on the condition that she not try any "funny business," and Taylor agreed . . . but suddenly had second thoughts.

"You wouldn't hold me responsible for what I did in my sleep, would you?"

But he just pulled her close and grumbled, "You bet I would, you little sneak. Now, sleep." And she did.

Backstage, O'Brien gave her a quick, hard kiss and said, "No way to miss, babe," before he left her.

The excitement was killing. It was wonderful. She had to throw up.

She felt much better afterward. In fact, she felt fantastic.

She stood in place, blackout, curtain, white light. It began.

She felt the flow of action, of dialogue, take her, and ceased to measure a reaction.

They applauded and applauded. She was dazed through curtain calls. Someone gave her roses. Her eyes sought O'Brien in the wings and found Rhea and O'Malley smiling at her. As the curtains finally closed she saw O'Brien coming toward her pushing a wheelbarrow full of daisies, sneezing all the way.

Five feet from her he straightened, held out his arms, and said, "C'mere, you!"

She laughed out loud with sheer pleasure before she looked at her big, watery-eyed idiot. The sight made her swallow hard and hold out her own arms in pantomime of his. Her world was full.

Then, an odd gleam in her eye, she spoke to him in some sort of code, laughing all the while.

"*Do* da!"

Only a sneeze answered her.

"Zippo?" she tried, holding onto her dignity.

"Red," he bellowed. "*C'mere!*"

And, as she snuggled deeply in his arms, she lifted her lips to his ear and murmured, "My *favorite* frog!"

He merely harrumphed.

THE EDITOR'S CORNER

There is a very special treat in store for you next month from Bantam Books. Although not a LOVESWEPT, I simply must tell you about Celeste DeBlasis's magnificent hardcover novel **WILD SWAN**. Celeste has demonstrated to us all what a superb storyteller and gifted writer she is in such works as **THE PROUD BREED** and **THE TIGER'S WOMAN**. So, you can imagine with what relish I approached the reading of the galleys of her latest novel one weekend not too long ago. I couldn't put **WILD SWAN** down. I wrapped myself in this touching, exciting, involving story and was darned sorry when I'd finished that last paragraph. I'll bet you, too, will find this epic tale riveting. Spanning decades and sweeping from England's West Country during the years of the Napoleonic Wars to the beautiful but trouble-shadowed countryside of Maryland, **WILD SWAN** is a fascinating story centered around an unforgettable heroine, Alexandria Thiane. And the very heart of the work is an exploration of love in its many facets—passionate, enduring, transcendent. **WILD SWAN** is a grand story, by a grand writer. Do remember to ask your bookseller for this novel; I really don't think you'll want to wait until it comes out in paperback!

And now to the LOVESWEPTS you can look forward to reading next month.

In **TOUCH THE HORIZON** (LOVESWEPT #59) Iris Johansen gives us the tender story of Billie Callahan, the touching young madcap introduced last month in **CAPTURE THE RAINBOW**. On her own at last in the mysterious desert land of Sedikhan, Billie is driving her jeep toward a walled city when she is rescued from a terrifying sandstorm by a dashing figure on a black stallion. He sweeps her into his arms and steals

(continued)

her heart. Shades of the Arabian Nights! Those of you who've read many of Iris's books in the past will recognize some old friends and thrill to the golden-haired, blue-eyed hero whose kisses send Billie spinning off the edge of the world. This lively adventure tale may be Iris's most wonderful love story to date! Don't be too frustrated now that I haven't given you the hero's name. It's a surprise from Iris. And do let me tantalize you with just a few words: he's a poignant character introduced in an early work and through letters I know many of you have complimented Iris on his creation, rooted for him, taken him into your hearts. At the end of Chapter One, you'll know his name and, I suspect, you'll be cheering!

One of the pleasures of publishing LOVESWEPT romances is discovering talented new writers, wonderful storytellers who bring us their unique insights into the special relationships between men and women. This month we're introducing two of our most exciting new discoveries: first, BJ James, whose novel **WHEN YOU SPEAK LOVE** (LOVESWEPT #60) offers an intense, dramatic and touching romance with a truly endearing cast of characters. While it was heartbreaking tragedy that brought Jake Caldwell and Kelly O'Brian together, what followed was the nurturing of a special kind of love between two people who've longed for closeness but have never known its intimate joy. We think you'll agree that BJ's first novel for LOVESWEPT is beautifully and sensitively written, a truly memorable debut.

Our second "debutante" brings a delicious sense of humor to her first LOVESWEPT romance. Joan Elliott Pickart may be **BREAKING ALL THE RULES** (LOVE-SWEPT #61) in this irresistible confection, but you'll be delighted to join in the fun! Blaze Holland and Taylor Shay both vowed they weren't looking to fall in love that wintry day in New York City, but the stormy weather wasn't the only thing beyond their control. Blaze is one of the most unforgettable heroines we've seen in a long time—and Taylor the perfect foil for her headlong tumble into the arms of love. These two give a new romantic flavor to the notion of popcorn as a potential aphrodisiac! Was falling in love always this much fun?

When you're looking for someone very special, what's the fastest way to find him? If you're Pepper, the resourceful and constantly astonishing heroine of **PEPPER'S WAY** (LOVESWEPT #62), you place an innocently provocative ad in your local newspaper that's sure to compel the perfect candidate to respond! Kay Hooper has done it again with this beguiling and whimsical tale of loving pursuit. Thor Spicer answers the ad and suddenly finds himself the object of Pepper's tireless fascination. He's never met a dynamo like this lady before, and his goose is definitely cooked! **PEPPER'S WAY** is a delightfully romantic story, brimming with the unpredictable twists and turns you've come to relish in each new book by Kay Hooper. Perhaps I shouldn't reveal this, but I've always fantasized about having certain of the unusual talents that Pepper reveals to Thor and his friend Cody in this absolutely wonderful love story!

Whew! September positively sizzles with romance that won't fade at summer's end. It's great to know you'll be there to share it with us as the leaves turn those glorious shades of red and gold!

With warm good wishes,

Sincerely,

Carolyn Nichols

Carolyn Nichols
  Editor
LOVESWEPT
Bantam Books, Inc.
666 Fifth Avenue
New York, NY 10103

WILD SWAN

Celeste De Blasis

Author of THE PROUD BREED

Spanning decades and sweeping from England's West Country in the years of the Napoleonic Wars to the beauty of Maryland's horse country—a golden land shadowed by slavery and soon to be ravaged by war—here is a novel richly spun of authentically detailed history and sumptuous romance, a rewarding woman's story in the grand tradition of A WOMAN OF SUBSTANCE. WILD SWAN is the story of Alexandria Thaine, youngest and unwanted child of a bitter mother and distant father—suddenly summoned home to care for her dead sister's children. Alexandria—for whom the brief joys of childhood are swiftly forgotten . . . and the bright fire of passion nearly extinguished.

Buy WILD SWAN, on sale in hardcover August 15, 1984, wherever Bantam Books are sold, or use the handy coupon below for ordering: